*Here's what reviewers
are saying about*
TO HAVE AND TO HOLD

"At last a line that goes beyond the 'happily ever after' ending.... What really makes these books special is their view of marriage as an exciting, vibrant blossoming of love out of the courtship stage. Clichés such as the 'other woman' are avoided, as family backgrounds are beautifully interwoven with plot to create a very special romantic glow."

—Melinda Helfer, *Romantic Times*

"At last, a series of honest, convincing and delightfully reassuring stories about the joys of matrimonial love. Men and women who sometimes doubt that a happy marriage can be achieved should read these books."

—Vivien Jennings, *Boy Meets Girl*

"I am extremely impressed by the high quality of writing within this new line. Romance readers who have been screaming for stories of romance, sensuality, deep commitment and love will not want to miss this line. I feel that this line will become not only a favorite of mine but of the millions of romance readers."

—Terri Busch, *Heart Line*

## "Adam..."

"Mmmm..."

"Are you asleep?"

One eye opened and peered at her. It took him only a moment to decipher the reason for Kate's bewitching smile. A quiver of anticipation ran through him as he stretched slowly. "Maybe."

The teasing gleam in his crystal blue gaze emboldened her. Shifting slightly, she let the tips of her breasts brush against him. Her deep brown eyes grew cloudy with passion as her lips sought the hollow at the base of his throat. "It would be a shame if you are."

"Oh," Adam parried huskily, "why's that?"

"Because..." Her hands slid down to his lean hips and sinewy thighs. "Then you'd miss this..." Her tongue darted out, savoring the faintly salty taste of his skin. "And this..."

Dear Reader:

Last month we were delighted to announce the arrival of TO HAVE AND TO HOLD, the thrilling new romance series that takes you into the world of married love. This month we're pleased to report that letters of praise and enthusiasm are pouring in daily. TO HAVE AND TO HOLD is clearly off to a great start!

TO HAVE AND TO HOLD is the first and only series that portrays the joys and heartaches of marriage. Its unique concept makes it significantly different from the other lines now available to you, and it offers stories that meet the high standards set by SECOND CHANCE AT LOVE. TO HAVE AND TO HOLD offers all the compelling romance, exciting sensuality, and heartwarming entertainment you expect.

We think you'll love TO HAVE AND TO HOLD—and that you'll become the kind of loyal reader who is making SECOND CHANCE AT LOVE an ever-increasing success. Read about love affairs that last a lifetime. Look for three TO HAVE AND TO HOLD romances each and every month, as well as six SECOND CHANCE AT LOVE romances each month. We hope you'll read and enjoy them all. And please keep writing! Your thoughts about our books are very important to us.

Warm wishes,

*Ellen Edwards*

Ellen Edwards
TO HAVE AND TO HOLD
The Berkley Publishing Group
200 Madison Avenue
New York, N.Y. 10016

# To Have and to Hold

# GILDED SPRING
# JENNY BATES

**SECOND CHANCE AT LOVE BOOK**

**GILDED SPRING**

Copyright © 1983 by Jenny Bates

Distributed by The Berkley Publishing Group

All rights reserved. No part of this publication may be reproduced or transmitted in any form or by any means, electronic or mechanical, including photocopy, recording, or any information storage and retrieval system, without permission in writing from the publisher.

Requests for permission to make copies of any part of the work should be mailed to: Permissions, To Have and to Hold, The Berkley Publishing Group, 200 Madison Avenue, New York, NY 10016.

First edition published November 1983

First printing

"Second Chance at Love," the butterfly emblem, and "To Have and to Hold" are trademarks belonging to Jove Publications, Inc.

Printed in the United States of America

To Have and to Hold books are published by
The Berkley Publishing Group
200 Madison Avenue, New York, NY 10016

# 1

KATE TURNED OVER slowly in bed and opened her eyes. From the strong eastern light streaming through the high window she could tell that it was still early. Even without glancing at the alarm clock, she knew she could safely go back to sleep for a while. It took her a moment to realize why she didn't want to. Adam's long, hard body nestled against her own had awakened other needs.

A smile curved her sleep-softened mouth as she regarded her husband lovingly. His thick chestnut hair was mussed, and a night's growth of beard roughened the planes and hollows of his face. Beneath slanting brows, his eyes were closed, but she had no difficulty imagining their startlingly light-blue gaze.

Moving closer, she trailed a finger along the bridge of his nose, broken years before during a street fight in the Appalachian mining town he had long since left behind. His nose gave a rugged set to his features. His lips were slightly parted. Beneath the sheet and thin blanket, which were his only covering, she could see the rhythmic rise and fall of his powerful chest.

He had been working so hard lately that she hesitated to wake him. But the signs of tension and fatigue she had noted the night before were gone. After almost eight hours of sleep, he looked well rested and more than capable of enjoying what she had in mind.

Propping herself up on an elbow, she pushed her dark blond hair out of the way and touched a feather-light kiss to his mouth. Her hand trailed gently up his arm and shoulder to stroke the silken curls at the nape of his neck.

"Adam..."

"Mmmm..."

"Are you asleep?"

One eye opened and peered at her. It took him only a moment to decipher the reason for her bewitching smile. A quiver of anticipation ran through him as he stretched slowly. "Maybe."

The teasing gleam in his crystal blue gaze emboldened her. Shifting slightly, she let the tips of her breasts brush against him. The thick mat of hair covering his torso made her nipples harden instantly. Desire flared through her. Her deep brown eyes grew cloudy with passion as her lips sought the hollow at the base of his throat. "It would be a shame if you are."

"Oh," Adam parried huskily, "why's that?"

"Because..." Her hands slid down to his lean hips and sinewy thighs, taut with the beginnings of his own desire. "Then you'd miss this..." Her tongue darted out, savoring the faintly salty taste of his skin. At thirty-five he was ruggedly attractive in an utterly masculine, supremely arousing way. It required all her willpower to continue the slow, languorous seduction.

"And this..." Moving her leg just enough to confirm the effectiveness of her caresses, she laughed

# Gilded Spring

softly. Adam might be pretending to be still half-asleep, but his body said otherwise. A delicious sense of womanly power provoked her to test the limits of his endurance.

He bore it as long as he could. The covers were tangled at the foot of the bed and their bodies shone with a light sheen of perspiration before his self-control broke. A low growl rumbled from him as he reached for her.

Though he now spent his days behind a desk on Wall Street, his reflexes remained as finely honed as they had been when he was working in the mines to put himself through college. The arms that closed around her were implacable in their strength, yet utterly gentle. Kate barely had a chance to catch her breath before she was tumbled onto her back, her slender length covered by her husband's far larger and more powerful body.

From the first time they were together, Adam had known how to bring her to a peak of exquisite pleasure. Over the years his understanding of her had grown so that their lovemaking could be almost frightening in its intensity.

Kate felt herself dissolving, her grip on reality fading, as his hands and mouth moved over her. He teased her sometimes about being so quiet in bed, and it was true that she was never especially vocal. But she could not hold back the moan that broke from her as he traced patterns of delight down the slender column of her throat, across her silken shoulders, into the hollow at the base of her throat.

When his tongue at last flicked across her swollen nipples, she moaned again. Her hands, tangled in his hair, tried to draw him closer. But Adam held back. He brought her to a peak of near-painful rapture before at last driving deep within the moist warmth she so ardently offered.

Moving strongly yet carefully, he quickly established a rhythm she could not resist. The first teasing hint of exquisite pleasure made her tremble. She chased the sensation, her fingers caught in the crisp sheet and her breath coming fast. Liquid fire flashed through her. A deep, irresistible spasm began in her belly, moving up and out to explode at the furthest reaches of consciousness. They crested together in a joyful melding that left them both limp with delight.

Long moments later Adam moved to her side. His voice shook slightly as he murmured, "I'll probably die young, but at least I'll be smiling."

Kate laughed softly. The totally unrestrained response his lovemaking provoked never failed to astonish her. She felt as though her body were floating on a soft, warm cloud high above the rest of the world. All the problems and concerns of everyday life had faded to insignificance.

Nestling into the curve of his arm, she smiled contentedly. "You're a great source of inspiration. Even asleep, you're irresistible."

"That's true," Adam agreed, teasing her.

"Not to mention modest."

"The list of my virtues is endless."

Kate snorted. "A regular Superman."

Laughing, Adam turned over suddenly, carrying her with him. Pinned to the mattress, she could only stare up at him as he said, "You seemed to think so a few minutes ago."

# Gilded Spring 5

"I was just being polite."

"Like hell."

"I didn't want to bruise your manly ego."

"Watch yourself, woman," he said, growling menacingly.

"Look at me—I'm terrified."

Sighing, Adam flopped back down beside her. "That's what I get for marrying a liberated woman. No respect, even in bed."

Kate's mouth quirked remorselessly. Her hand traced the thick mat of hair covering his chest down over his flat abdomen to his groin. Her nails raked him lightly. "Is that what you really want—respect?"

Adam groaned softly. "Why didn't I meet you when I was eighteen?"

"I wouldn't have done you much good, since I was only twelve."

"I'll bet you were driving the boys nuts even then."

"Maybe you're right," Kate admitted. "I do remember Sherri telling me once not to get in the backseat with one of them."

"Smart woman, your older sister."

"You just say that because she liked you the moment you walked in the door."

"Sure she did. She knew she could stop worrying about what kind of mischief you'd get into once you were my problem."

Kate took a playful swat at him. "That's not exactly the way I remember it."

Catching both her hands in one of his, Adam held them firmly as he grinned at her. "Oh no?"

"Absolutely not. I seem to recall you pleading with me to make an honest man of you."

"I did say something about marriage maybe being a good idea," Adam acknowledged. "But only because I couldn't stand the idea of your going out with anyone else once I'd taken you to bed."

"As though I would have," she scoffed gently. Her mood turned suddenly serious as she gazed at him lovingly. "I'd have had to be crazy to give any other man the time of day, and you know it."

Adam smiled as he released her hands. His eyes lingered on her flushed face and form. She was so lovely in both body and spirit that sometimes he could hardly believe she was his.

With the high rate of divorce, it was impossible not to be aware of how risky marriage could be. Yet not once in five years had he ever regretted their relationship. The conviction that they belonged together had grown steadily from the moment they'd met. Sometimes it was difficult for him to express his feelings, but he knew beyond the slightest doubt that she was the center of his life.

A tender smile curved his mouth as he watched her eyes close languorously. "You're not falling asleep, are you?" he asked.

"What if I am?"

Adam chuckled softly. "I hate to tell you this, sweetheart, but it's later than you think."

Reluctantly Kate glanced at the clock. Her eyes shot open as she realized he was right. Their lovemaking had made her lose all track of time. If they didn't get out of bed now, they would both be late for work.

Sighing, she pushed back the covers and stood up. Adam eyed her nudity with frank appreciation. "On the other hand, it's not polite to go rushing off..."

"Duty calls." Glancing back at him over her bare shoulder, she added provocatively, "Besides, I wouldn't want to wear you out."

A pillow hit her square on the buttocks as she dashed for the bathroom. She stepped into the shower and reluctantly soaped away traces of their lovemaking while resisting the temptation to linger under the stream of soothing water.

Adam was standing at the sink shaving when she emerged. They paused only long enough for a quick kiss before changing places. Moments later the sound of his deep baritone filled the misty air.

"Luciano Pavarotti has nothing to worry about," Kate said with a groan.

"What's that? I can't hear you."

"I was just commenting on the brilliant operatic career you foolishly denied the world."

"You're just jealous 'cause you can't carry a tune with a wheelbarrow." Launching unrepentently into a rendition of "Celeste Aida," he sent her scurrying from the dressing room.

Wrapped in a terry-cloth robe, she brushed out the dark blond hair that fell smoothly to her shoulders and quickly completed her usual makeup routine. Her eyes had an added glow, and her gently curved mouth was slightly swollen from Adam's kisses. A warm flush stained her high-boned cheeks and the bridge of her slightly upturned nose.

Wishing it were the weekend, so that they could have lingered in bed, she straightened and headed for the closet to select pleated trousers in camel wool, a matching jacket, and a silk print blouse that were well suited to her slender but nicely curved figure. Low-heeled Italian leather pumps added little to her five feet eight inches, which was tall by some standards but still left her well short of Adam's six feet plus.

She was downstairs in the kitchen starting breakfast by the time he finished dressing and came to help. Showered and shaved, wearing a crisp white shirt and gray slacks that matched the jacket he slung over a chair, he looked ready to take on the world. His movements were swift and assured as he slid muffins onto plates and poured two large mugs of coffee. Glancing up, he caught her watching him and grinned.

"Something on your mind, Mrs. Remington?"

"Oh, I was just thinking that as husbands go, you're not so bad." Her eyes widened slightly as she noticed the eggs and several slices of bacon he was fixing. "A little expensive to feed, maybe..."

"And whose fault is it that I worked up such a healthy appetite?"

Pulling place mats from a drawer, Kate leaned forward to kiss him lightly. "Mine, I guess." Generously she added, "But I have to admit it was worth it."

Keeping one eye on the stove, Adam patted her rump. "Get the table set, woman, before I decide I'm not too hungry to teach a sassy dame what happens when she gets too big for her britches."

Seated across from him at the butcher-block table that occupied one corner of the large, airy kitchen, she swiped a forkful of scrambled eggs from his plate and sighed. "I'll probably outgrow these slacks if you keep fixing breakfasts like this."

Adam grinned. "If that happens, I promise to work it off you." He hesitated, then asked, "You're going

# Gilded Spring

to see Dr. Thorpe today, aren't you?"

"Yes, after work." She deliberately kept her answer brief, hoping he would take the hint and drop the subject. They had already discussed her reason for seeing the gynecologist. There was no point in going into it again, at least not until she had a clearer idea of how much of a problem, if any, she had developed.

"Speaking of work, any chance of getting a break sometime soon?"

She smiled, appreciating his tact. "Why, what did you have in mind?"

"A vacation. It's been quite a while."

"I guess it has. Any place in particular you want to go?"

"Just somewhere quiet, maybe on the water. Even a weekend would be nice."

"I guess so..."

"You don't sound real taken with the idea."

"It's not that. Lately I just seem to have a hard time getting very excited about anything." She broke off, well aware that with them both due at work shortly, this was not the time to bring up the vague unease that had recently been bothering her. Collecting their empty plates, she sought some way to put a quick end to the unpleasant topic she had inadvertently introduced.

Sensing her predicament, he helped her out. "Oh, I don't know about that. You seemed pretty excited this morning."

Kate laughed and took a playful swat at him with the dishtowel. "Cad! A gentleman would never bring that up."

A wicked gleam shone in his eyes. "What about

what a certain lady brought up? There I was, sleeping peacefully, minding my own business, and—"

"Want me to promise not to do it again?" she asked demurely.

"No way! In fact, if we didn't have to go out tonight, I'd be happy to show you just how much I approve of being seduced."

The reminder that they were due at Carol and Ray's that evening also recalled other obligations. "I've got a creative meeting at four," Kate said, "but it shouldn't run late. Davey's birthday is coming up, so I'll pick up a present for him after work."

"Fine, but remember, he's only four. Try not to choose something you really want to play with yourself."

"He always likes what we give him," she insisted, defending her tendency to spoil their godchild. Selecting gifts for him gave her an excuse to wander through toy stores.

"He likes the boxes they come in," Adam corrected. Gazing down at her gently, he added, "With a half-dozen nieces and nephews, you ought to know enough about kids to realize that."

"I've been away from them for quite a while," she pointed out softly. "After all, I'll be thirty next month."

He drew back slightly, staring at her in mock dismay. "If I'd remembered that this morning, I would have gone easier on you. At your age, you need to conserve your strength."

"If we weren't already late," she retorted, "I'd show you who went easy on whom."

"Promises, promises." Slipping into his jacket, he eyed her teasingly. "Maybe I should whisk you off to some secluded island where I can have my wicked way with you."

"Now that's a vacation I could get excited about," she assured him warmly.

Outside on the front steps they paused for a moment. The sky above Brooklyn Heights was brilliantly clear. A soft breeze wafted over the river from the direction of Manhattan. Instead of the usual acrid reminders of too many people and too much traffic crammed into too little space, it carried the pleasant, earthy scents of fertile soil and burgeoning plants.

The branches of trees planted at regular intervals along the sidewalk shone with a soft green haze. As if in stubborn defiance of urban life, buds had appeared. On patchwork squares of lawn, daffodils were blooming. Robins had arrived seemingly overnight to dart among the flowers.

Up and down the street of well-maintained row houses, people were taking note of the sudden change of seasons. Men and women stopped on the way to their offices to sniff the air and smile. A few even nodded to one another, sharing a moment that came all too rarely in their hectic existences.

Kate was watching a stern-faced gentleman cheerfully greet a young mother and child when Adam draped an arm around her waist and pulled her closer. She inhaled sharply as he kissed her deeply.

For a long moment they stood locked together, heedless of any passing neighbors who might notice them. As abruptly as he had begun, Adam ended the caress. He stepped back a little, grinning down at her. "Let's not stay late at Carol and Ray's. Okay?"

Kate's eyes widened. After five years they rarely

made love more than once a day. Maybe Adam's arousal had something to do with the arrival of spring. "Feeling your oats?" she murmured against his mouth.

He laughed in acknowledgment. "Any objections?"

She shook her head, smiling in full agreement with his intentions. Hand in hand they walked to the bus stop and boarded, when it arrived minutes later. Traffic was as congested as usual, but neither of them noticed. Both were immersed in the paperwork they had brought home the night before. Adam's stop came first. He kissed Kate lightly before getting off.

She watched him through the window as he strode down the street toward his office. Sunlight turned his thick chestnut hair to gold. The agile strength of his body was evident in every step he took. Pride mingled with remembered pleasure as she savored the knowledge that he was hers. Only when the bus started up again did she manage to turn her thoughts to her own job and what promised to be a trying day.

## 2

DESPITE KATE'S CONCERN that she might get stuck at the office and have to cancel her appointment with Dr. Thorpe, she was able to leave in plenty of time to get uptown before the worst of the home-bound traffic hit. With five minutes to spare, the taxi left her in front of the Park Avenue apartment building that housed the offices of several psychologists, obstetricians, plastic surgeons, and other specialists.

One of the reasons Kate had chosen Dr. Thorpe was that she rarely kept patients waiting. Kate had barely sat down in the pleasantly furnished reception area before she was ushered in to chat with the doctor before being examined.

Eloise Thorpe was a Harvard M.D. whose credentials included residencies at Bellevue and Mt. Sinai hospitals. At forty-eight the attractive auburn-haired woman had a thriving practice specializing in obstetrical care. She was the third gynecologist Kate had visited in New York. The first two had been men. One had called her honey and made it clear he didn't like to answer questions. The other had been rough, turning what should have been a painless examination into an ordeal. A friend had recommended Dr. Thorpe three years ago. Kate had seen her regularly since then and had no urge to change doctors again.

Consulting her file, the older woman said, "Your regular checkup isn't for a couple of months, so there must be something special going on. What's the problem?"

"I'm not sure, exactly," Kate admitted. "My periods were always relatively painless up until a few months ago, when they became increasingly uncomfortable. There seems to be more involved than ordinary cramps. With my last period or two I've had severe pain all the way around to my lower back. I thought I should come to see you before it happened again."

"I'm glad you did. My job would be a lot simpler if patients didn't ignore symptoms until they became unbearable. Let me just get a bit more information, and then we can see what's going on."

After answering a dozen or so questions about her general health, Kate followed Dr. Thorpe into one of the examining rooms. Wrapped in a paper robe, she lay back, staring up at the ceiling and trying to relax. Her confidence that she was in good hands was reconfirmed as the doctor gently and swiftly performed the necessary check.

"There's a slight inflammation," Dr. Thorpe explained. "Nothing serious, but tied in with the pain you've been having, it's enough to make me suspect you may be building up to something much more severe." After hesitating a moment she said, "Why don't you get dressed and meet me back in the office. We'll talk there."

Kate nodded. She had half-expected the doctor to tell her that what she had been experiencing was just

## Gilded Spring

a fluke and there was no reason to be concerned. Instead it looked as though the situation could not be dismissed so readily.

Seeing Kate's worried expression as she returned to the office, Dr. Thorpe said, "Don't look so glum. What I have to tell you isn't really all that bad. The condition you're developing isn't particularly uncommon among women in their late twenties or beyond who haven't had children." Glancing down at the file, she asked, "Am I right in believing you have never been pregnant?"

Kate nodded. "Adam and I have talked about it, of course. More frequently lately. But we still haven't decided."

"Well, I think you may want to discuss it again. The inflammation of your womb might be the beginning of a potentially serious problem called endometriosis. What that means basically is that you're not shedding the lining of the uterus each month as thoroughly as you should be. Too much of it is remaining inside you, to the point where it's beginning to cause problems elsewhere. That's why you're having pain in your lower back."

"Can you treat it?"

"Yes, but the best course of treatment is also the simplest: Get pregnant. Since you won't menstruate for nine months while you're pregnant, your body will have plenty of time to correct the problem. And once you begin again, changes in your body that are a normal aftereffect of pregnancy should prevent it from recurring."

"But if there's something wrong with my uterus, is it safe for me to conceive?"

"At this point, yes. Later on it might be more difficult. Endometriosis can cause scarring around the ovarian tubes, which could prevent conception."

Kate swallowed hard. She was so unaccustomed to having health problems of any kind that what the doctor was telling her took some getting used to. She was still trying to assimilate it all when she left the office a short time later and, after stopping to buy a present for Davey, headed home.

"So how did it go today?" Adam asked a short time later as he dropped his shirt in the hamper. They were both in the bathroom, getting ready for the dinner party. Kate had stripped down to her bra and panties and was busy freshening her makeup. Adam's gaze lingered on her rounded bottom as he ran a hand over his lean jaw, wondering if he really needed to shave again.

"Fine ... I guess. I got the Femme account."

Adam looked up swiftly. "That's terrific! I know you really wanted it."

It was true she had hoped to be named chief copywriter for what promised to be one of the most exciting and well-financed cosmetics campaigns ever launched. But her meeting with Dr. Thorpe had taken the edge off her elation.

Correctly guessing the reason for her seeming lack of enthusiasm, Adam closed his arms around her. He tenderly kissed the nape of her neck. "Want to tell me what the doctor had to say?"

Kate sighed. She knew she had to tell him; they didn't have the kind of relationship in which they kept such things to themselves. But she didn't want to

# Gilded Spring 17

worry him. As lightly as she could, she said, "Dr. Thorpe thinks I should get pregnant."

Adam turned her around in his arms and gazed down at her. "Because you're almost thirty?"

"No, not exactly..." Briefly she explained what the doctor had told her. By the time she finished, Adam was frowning with concern.

"This sounds really serious."

"It isn't," she assured him quickly. "Or at least it doesn't have to be if it's taken care of soon. There are alternative treatments—hormones, that kind of thing. But having a baby seems to be nature's own solution to the problem." Hesitantly she added, "We have talked about starting a family. You seemed to like the idea, at least in theory."

"I do," Adam quickly confirmed. "So maybe we'd better discuss it some more, soon."

Kate smiled a bit shakily She wasn't prepared for the sudden transformation of what had been a pleasant possibility for the future into an immediate urgency. But the anxiety she saw in Adam's eyes overrode her own concern. "Don't worry about me," she said gently. "You'll frown and get wrinkles and then I'll have to look for a younger man."

"I've already got wrinkles, or hadn't you noticed?"

"Well, maybe a few..." She touched a gentle finger to the corner of one eye, where his tanned skin was slightly crinkled. Impishly she added, "But what I really like are your gray hairs."

*"My what?"*

Pulling his head down, Kate surveyed the glistening strands that curled slightly at her touch. "Oh, yes, I can see lots of them." As his hands tightened warningly around her waist, she amended, "Make that a few." Choosing to ignore his irate growl, she went on blithely. "There are even a couple on your chest."

"Undoubtedly one for each year I've spent with a certain woman."

"You think so? Let's count..." Her hands stroked down the muscles of his back to his narrow hips as she attempted to wiggle free of him.

"Let's not," Adam corrected, letting her go. "Not if we want to get to Ray and Carol's anytime tonight."

"Spoilsport." Pouting Kate picked up her brush and tried to restore order to her tangled hair while Adam glanced ruefully down at himself.

"I must be going through a second adolescence," he muttered, not without a touch of smugness.

Kate laughed deep in her throat. "You do seem a wee bit more—vigorous these days."

His voice was muffled as he pulled on a light blue sweater that was the same shade as his eyes. "You know what we say on the Street. When the market goes up, so does—"

"Never mind," she interrupted hastily. "Like you said, we're due at Ray and Carol's."

Adam grinned as his head emerged from the turtleneck. "You just want to get there in time to play with Davey."

Kate didn't deny it. A few minutes later they left to stroll the half-dozen blocks to their friends' apartment. The neighboring brownstone was similar to Kate and Adam's. Much of the original interior remained, including ornamental plasterwork on the high ceilings, intricately carved mantels, and rosewood doors.

Carol and Ray owned what had been the parlor

floor, fronted by a huge bay window that faced south. Flourishing Boston and asparagus ferns hung in front of the window, and Carol had recently started a small herb garden that appeared to be doing nicely. She had a knack for nurturing that extended from plants to friends. From the moment the front door opened, Kate and Adam were engulfed by a warm, welcoming hominess that seemed guaranteed to soothe even the most frazzled visitor.

"It's so good to see you," Carol exclaimed as the women touched cheeks and the men shook hands. "It's been quite a while."

"Not really." Kate laughed and hugged her friend. "It just seems longer because we've missed your cooking so much."

The enticing aromas of freshly baked bread and subtly spiced chicken drifted in from the kitchen, making Kate's mouth water.

"How do you stay so slender?" she asked petite Carol, who was wearing an ankle-length tartan skirt and an aqua sweater that matched her eyes. Straight chestnut hair hung halfway down her back, framing a gamin face. At twenty-eight, Carol could easily be mistaken for being ten years younger. "If I cooked like you do, I'd weigh a ton," Kate said.

"I can't imagine you getting fat," Carol told her loyally, guiding Kate and Adam into the living room. "You work much too hard to gain weight."

"Carol claims that after she cooks something she loses interest in it," Ray said teasingly, draping an arm around his wife's shoulders.

He was a tall, slender man of thirty-five with sandy hair and a freckled complexion. A shock of hair fell across his broad forehead, and his clothes never seemed to fit quite right, as though he were always outgrowing them. But he exuded an air of solid stability that was particularly reassuring in light of his profession as a nuclear engineer.

Kate knew that Ray had risen quickly within his company, in part because of his ability to explain complex ideas in terms the public could both understand and accept. In recent years he had traveled to many cities to speak to community groups. But his life centered around his wife and son, and he tried to be home whenever possible.

Davey resembled Ray closely. Clad in bright yellow pajamas, the four-year-old boy was busy constructing an elaborate tower of wooden blocks in the cheerfully chaotic living room. Kate doubted he would recognize her and Adam, since he hadn't seen them in months. But there was no shyness in the chubby arms that reached up to her or the sloppy kiss that landed squarely on her cheek. "Hi, Aunt Kate," he said. "You going to have dinner with us?"

Kate hoisted him onto her lap, liking the way his sturdy little body felt against her own. "You bet," she said. "Your Uncle Adam and I have missed you, so we thought we'd come and visit for a while."

"Did you bring me anything?"

Adam laughed. "He's got your number," he told Kate. "Four years old and already he knows you're a pushover." His tone was indulgent, as much for Kate as the child.

"Go look in my bag," she told Davey, watching as he scampered across the floor to delve for treasure. The brightly colored puzzle she had bought for him

## Gilded Spring 21

was wrapped in shiny paper. Davey tore it off swiftly, held up his prize to examine it, and chortled with delight.

"Do you think you can put it together?" Adam asked.

"Uh-huh. This one is easy," Davey informed him matter-of-factly.

He flopped down on the floor, his attention focused on the multicolor puzzle pieces clasped in his dimpled hands.

"That should keep him out of mischief for a while," Carol murmured appreciatively as she set out raw vegetables and a blue cheese dip. "God bless anything that does that!"

Kate laughed, knowing full well that Carol adored her small son and did nothing to discourage his boundless energy. She did, however, enjoy a few hours to herself each day now that he was enrolled in a preschool down the block. The two women chatted briefly about the neighborhood as Adam helped Ray fix drinks.

Half an hour after their arrival, when a good dent had been put in the blue cheese dip, Carol announced it was Davey's bedtime. He protested briefly, but his eyes were already closing as Kate accompanied Carol upstairs and helped tuck him in. The sight of his tiny figure fast asleep with his teddy bear clutched tightly to his chest did odd things to her. Unbidden, the thought rose of how she would feel if he were her own.

She was still mulling that idea over when they all sat down to dinner. Carol had outdone herself with a delicious chicken paprikash accompanied by loaves of whole-wheat bread and a lettuce, mushroom, and bean sprout salad. Conversation revolved around recent news events. They were just getting into a spirited discussion about the outlook for business when the sound of small feet padding down the stairs interrupted them.

Clutching a scrap of blanket in one hand and the teddy bear in the other, Davey stared at them sleepy-eyed. "I'm thirsty," he mumbled. "Want some kitchen water."

The adults laughed. Kate remembered the distinction between bathroom and kitchen water from her own childhood. Ray started to rise to attend to his son, but to Kate's surprise, Adam beat him to it. "I'll take care of him," he said, taking Davey by the hand. "Come on, sport. You can show me where the cups are."

The little boy went with him trustingly. Kate stared after them as they disappeared through the swinging doors to the kitchen. It occurred to her that Adam would make a good father. In the rare times she saw him with children, he was always perfectly natural and at ease. There was a warmth about him to which children readily responded. They seemed to know he would both look after and entertain them.

Davey certainly enjoyed his company. He was all set to crawl up on Adam's lap when they returned, but Carol forestalled him. "Bed for you, young man," she said firmly.

Davey's tiny mouth pursed petulantly, but he didn't argue. Kate guessed that when his mother spoke in that tone, he knew she meant what she said.

When Carol had once again settled Davey down

and they had cleared the dishes away, Ray surprised them by producing a bottle of champagne to go with dessert. He uncorked it with a flourish and filled their glasses before finally satisfying their curiosity about what they were celebrating.

He drew his wife to him and smiled tenderly down at her. "Davey's going to have a sister or brother in about six months," he said, making no effort to mask his pride.

"That's wonderful!" Kate exclaimed. "You must be thrilled."

Carol laughed a little shakily. "I'll be thrilled when the morning sickness ends. I'm tired of having to keep dry biscuits and a bowl next to the bed."

Kate wasn't fooled. She knew that having a baby meant the world to both Carol and Ray. But she was startled by the stab of envy that shot through her. It was so intense as to be almost painful. There was an ache inside her that she had never felt before.

To distract herself, she teased Carol gently. "I don't know how you can complain about morning sickness. You look absolutely fantastic, as though you're blooming."

Carol snorted derisively. "That's one of the ways nature compensates for turning a woman into a blimp. In a few more months I'll say good-bye to my toes. Won't see them again for ages. You know, even your belly button disappears. The first time I was pregnant I was convinced I wouldn't get it back."

Ray just laughed, but Adam shook his head in amazement. "It must be an incredible experience," he said, "to know there's actually a new human being growing inside you. Someone who will live into the next century and do all sorts of things we can't even imagine."

"The really incredible part is when the baby is born," Carol said softly. "There aren't any words to describe it. We were lucky enough with Davey to have natural childbirth. Ray was with me, and he held Davey even before the cord was cut."

"Scared the daylights out of me," Ray admitted. "You see a movie that's supposed to prepare you, but nothing really does. When it happens, you're part of a miracle and you know it. Of course, this time," he added jokingly, "I'll be an old hand at it, and I probably won't be impressed at all."

Carol laughed with him. "Last time you almost fainted. Next time you probably will, especially if it's a girl."

"Are you hoping for a girl?" Kate asked.

Carol nodded. "It would be nice. But basically I just want the baby to be healthy. Nothing else matters." She glanced at the champagne in her hand. "This is a real treat for me. Since I found out I was pregnant, I've been trying not to have any alcohol. My doctor says I shouldn't smoke or drink, and he'd really like me to give up coffee, although he isn't sure that's harmful. Everyone has a different opinion about what pregnant women should and shouldn't do, and most of them contradict each other." She sighed. "Five years ago it was a lot simpler. Then I just took my vitamins, drank lots of milk, and waddled through it."

"Davey was born perfectly all right," Adam pointed out. "So why do you have to do anything different this time?"

Carol shrugged. "It's the responsibility, I guess. God forbid I didn't follow all the latest advice and something did go wrong. I don't think I could live with myself. Besides," she added hesitantly, "I'm five years older now. Childbearing gets harder as you go along."

Carol's words echoed in Kate's mind all evening. Her friend was two years younger than herself, yet she was already concerned about what her age would mean for her pregnancy. A clock seemed to be ticking inside her, Kate thought dismally, warning her that her options were running out. Once again she recalled how Adam had acted with Davey. He deserved to have children.

Carol commented on his easy accord with her son when the two women were alone briefly in the kitchen. "Some men are like that," she said gently. "They take to fatherhood without any apparent effort. Ray did. Even though he travels a lot, I never feel as though I have sole responsibility for Davey. I know we're bringing him up together. That can be very reassuring."

"I guess so," Kate murmured. "But don't you feel sometimes as though..." She hesitated, groping for the right words. "As though you're cut off from the whole rest of your life? I know that having Davey is fantastically rewarding, but it must also be incredibly demanding. He takes everything you have to give, doesn't he?"

"He sure does," Carol agreed ruefully. "Some days I'm so tired by the time he goes to bed that I feel like I'm going to fall down. He keeps me constantly on the go. When he was first born, there were several months when I didn't sleep more than three or four hours at a stretch. I was nursing, and he had to be fed often, so I forgot what it was like to sleep through the night. That gets to you after a while. I was so worn out that sometimes I'd just sit and cry.

"Oh, it gets better," she added quickly, seeing Kate's dismay. "The first week I was able to sleep really well I felt as though I'd been reborn. When he got through teething, I almost threw a party to celebrate. When he learned to feed himself, I was ecstatic." She laughed, remembering. "Don't ask me why I'm going through the whole thing all over again. The only way I can explain it is to say that you have to experience it yourself to understand. It's the most glorious, egotistical, rewarding experience a person can have."

"Egotistical?" Kate asked, trying to equate even the slightest degree of conceit with the grind Carol had just described.

"It's the ego trip to end all," her friend insisted. "There's this tiny scrap of humanity that's part of you. You've brought him into being. You're launching him into the world like some magnificently daring adventure. When I look at Davey and think of all the things he'll see and do, it makes me feel almost as though it will be happening to me. He gives me a tiny taste of immortality that you just can't beat."

You certainly couldn't beat Carol's enthusiasm, Kate thought as she and Adam walked home a while later. Carol was one woman who had no doubts about what she was doing. She had left a promising career in television journalism to devote herself to her family. She had sacrificed a great deal, knowing that when

## Gilded Spring 27

she did return to her profession she might have to start at the bottom and pay her dues all over again. Seeing her so vibrant and alive, Kate found it impossible to doubt that Carol had made the right choice. But that didn't mean Kate could make the transition nearly as well.

"I had a great time," Adam said as he unlocked the front door. "How about you?"

"I always do. Carol and Ray are good to be with."

"We should have them over soon. Before Carol gets too far along."

Kate nodded. She waited as he slid the inside chain into place and checked the bolts. They went upstairs together. In her nightgown, curled up on the bed, she was lost in her own thoughts as Adam undressed. When he joined her in bed, drawing her against him, she was silent until he murmured, "Sleepy?"

"Not really."

"That's good."

Kate laughed softly, pleasantly reminded of the interlude they had shared that morning. Adam stroked her gently, his touch reassuring. She snuggled closer to him.

They made love slowly and tenderly, drawing out their pleasure to the utmost. The absolute fulfillment they shared so lulled Kate that she had almost drifted off to sleep in Adam's arms when he suddenly murmured, "Davey's a terrific little boy, isn't he?"

"Yes..." She hesitated, not wanting him to think she wasn't interested in what he had to say, but unable to cope with what she was sure he was leading up to. "Adam, I know you want to talk about what the doctor said, but could we put it off just a little longer? What with one thing and another, I'm really worn out."

"Sure, honey," he assured her at once. His hand cupped her head gently, drawing her into a comforting embrace. "You go to sleep. We've got plenty of time to talk about that."

Kate let her breath out slowly, greatly relieved that he wasn't pressing her. Her eyes seemed to close of their own volition. She was only dimly aware of the lips that touched hers in tender salute as consciousness faded.

# 3

"WHAT DO YOU want to do today?" Adam asked lazily as he finished reading the business section of the Sunday *Times*.

"I don't know. What do you want to do?"

"I asked you first."

Absorbed by an article in the book review section about the growing popularity of paperback romances, Kate looked up distractedly. "We could—go for a walk." She glanced out the window at the bright spring day. "We haven't been to Central Park in a while."

"Maybe stop for brunch somewhere?"

"Sounds good."

When the last of the coffee was gone, they climbed out of bed, showered, and dressed. Though she appreciated comfortable weekend clothes as much as anyone, Kate couldn't help but grimace at the frayed pair of jeans and faded plaid shirt Adam selected. He'd had them for at least ten years and refused to part with them, despite her frequent hints that they were more than ready for the rag bag.

"Wearing your old bum outfit again?"

Adam nodded unrepentently. "You bet. They just don't make clothes like this anymore."

"Thank God for that."

Pretending to look hurt, he demanded, "What's wrong with them? They're clean, aren't they?"

"I suppose. It's hard to tell with so many wrinkles and bags." It never failed to amaze her that a man who demanded impeccable tailoring in the entire rest of his wardrobe would be so fond of an outfit that looked as though it had been slept in several times over.

"Listen, I'll have you know it's taken me quite a while to get these just the way I want them."

Kate couldn't help but laugh at his earnestness. She supposed there would always be some part of him that retained a little boy's enthusiasm for messy clothes, mud puddles, and garter snakes. At least he didn't insist on bringing the other two home.

Slipping an apricot suede jacket over her forest green sweater and chocolate brown slacks, she came to stand next to him. The mirror showed a highly attractive young woman whose casual dress in no way detracted from her natural elegance. At her side was a big, scruffy-looking man whose tangled hair, unshaven face, and decidedly tough features gave him a faintly menacing air.

A mischievous grin curved his sensual mouth as he acknowledged what an odd pair they made. Taking Kate's hand, he asked, "Do you remember that time in Bloomingdale's when the woman at the perfume counter thought I was some weirdo accosting you?"

As she locked the door behind them, she giggled. "I sure do. I also remember how her attitude changed when you decided I absolutely had to have an ounce of that outrageously expensive perfume you liked so much."

# Gilded Spring 31

"All of a sudden I was just eccentric instead of crazy."

They made the trip across the East River and uptown reminiscing about where his propensity for looking like something the cat dragged in had occasionally led them.

"I'll never forget that time you came to my office to pick me up on your day off. The next morning the receptionist asked if you really were my husband. She'd heard I was married to a stockbroker and figured you couldn't possibly have been him."

"What did you tell her?"

"That the stockbroker was my *other* husband, and that in my opinion every woman should have at least two."

Adam laughed so loudly that an older couple getting off the bus ahead of them turned to stare critically. Catching their eyes, Kate said firmly, "You can laugh now, but wait until we get back to the institution and I tell them what you've been up to today."

"What makes you think I'll let you take me back?" Adam retorted, falling in with her game.

"Now, Mr. Remington," Kate said soothingly, "you know that if you make any trouble you won't get time off for good behavior."

"Oh, I'm good, all right," he announced, leering at her. "Let's go find a nice big bush to hide behind, and I'll prove it to you."

The outraged gasp of their listeners followed them into the park as they both dissolved into laughter. "We're being really silly," Kate pointed out unnecessarily.

"Spring is the silly season. Didn't you know that?"

With her hand held snugly in his, she smiled archly. "I thought it was the season when a young man's fancy turned to you know what."

"No, tell me."

"Baseball."

"Not this man's fancy."

"So I've noticed," Kate teased, pausing to watch a squirrel scamper across the path. "Let's stop at the zoo to buy some peanuts."

Strolling past the pony cart track, they smiled at the squealing children lined up with tickets clutched in their hands. Kate remembered rides she had shared with her sister when the two of them had ventured into the city from the affluent Long Island suburb where they had grown up. She shook her head, thinking of how young they had been when they started roaming around on their own.

Only good luck had kept them from getting into serious trouble. Certainly their corporate-executive father and charity-club mother had been far too concerned with their own lives to be interested in their daughters'. They still were, Kate thought ruefully. She hadn't spoken with either parent in months and doubted if her sister Sherri had either.

Determined not to think about what was still a source of pain, Kate concentrated on watching the children. Their exuberance was infectious. She and Adam were laughing again as they stopped in front of the sea lions' pool, enjoying the antics of the two males and one female, who seemed greatly amused by the humans they were supposed to be entertaining.

As Adam went off to buy peanuts, Kate noticed a little girl visiting the zoo with her parents. The child,

## Gilded Spring

who couldn't have been more than three, clutched a balloon tightly as she stared enraptured at the sea lions. Her wide-eyed wonder recalled Adam's comment on how children could make the world seem new again.

Maybe that was what was wrong with her, Kate thought as she considered her recent lack of enthusiasm for everything from vacations to career advancement. Even when she'd been on her own in New York, after Sherri had gone off to California and married a wine grower, she had still found much to be happy about. The city, her independence, her first job after college had all excited her enormously. Now the only thing that gave her that heady rush of elation was Adam.

Being with him, loving him, thinking about their future together were all that really seemed to matter. Which was foolish, since her career was still very important to her, not simply for its financial contribution to their life-style but because so much of her sense of herself as a separate person stemmed from her professional accomplishments.

If she had thought there was any danger of losing her hard-won identity as a top advertising copywriter, she would have been dismayed. But she was as secure as anyone in that volatile field could be. She was secure enough to feel discontent. With professional and marital assurance had come the urge for something more. An as-yet-unfulfilled part of her was finally demanding attention.

And why not, she asked herself as she smiled at the little girl. After all, wasn't there a time to every purpose under heaven?

"You're far away," Adam murmured, slipping an

arm around her waist.

The eyes Kate turned to him were so tender that his own widened. Softly he asked, "What were you thinking about?"

"Having a baby."

"Oh... You mean because of what the doctor said?"

"That and because the idea has a certain appeal all its own. Don't you think so?"

Instead of answering directly, he said, "Just now when I went to get the peanuts, there was a little boy with his dad. They were having a really great time together. I got to thinking what it would be like..." As though embarrassed by the depth of his own feeling, he added, "Hell, for all I know the guy's divorced and only sees the kid on weekends."

"Maybe, but that's not the point. Our marriage is solid. We both know that. The question is, would we make good parents?"

"What do you think?"

"I think," she said softly, "that you keep batting the issue back to me rather than making up your own mind. That's not going to work. You have to decide for yourself how you feel about this before we can go any further."

Adam glanced at her ruefully. She had spoken gently, but he could not mistake the firmness in her words. Neither could he deny that she was right. Having been raised in the Appalachian back country predisposed him to think of childbearing as strictly women's business. But everything he had learned since then confirmed his instinctive belief that he both wanted and needed to take a full part in his child's upbringing, even before its conception.

"A guy I know at the office," he said slowly, "told me that if it were left to us men, probably no kids would ever get born."

Kate squeezed his arm gently. "Fortunately, it isn't. But you are a rather important part of it."

"He also said that if every man had to say right out that he wanted to become a father, the baby population would be guaranteed to decline sharply."

"Are you suggesting I should try to *guess* how you feel?"

"No, of course not." He was at a loss to explain what he meant. Somehow the thought of asking a woman to bear his child simply overwhelmed him. After a lifetime of besting challenges that many other men couldn't even face, he had at last found one that was beyond him.

Sensing his unease, Kate let the issue drop for the moment. They wandered through the park, finally emerging on Central Park West and heading toward Columbus Avenue, where a stretch of boutiques and restaurants were revitalizing Manhattan's Upper West Side. Over a brunch of eggs Benedict, Bloody Marys, and salads, Kate coaxed Adam into telling her how things were going at the office. He spoke so rarely of his work that it was difficult for her always to know how he felt about it.

But for once he opened up on the subject, regaling her with stories about mad scrambles to buy hot stocks and dump those that had suddenly turned sour, about investors who risked fortunes on the strength of horoscopes and tarot-card readings; and the old guard of the Street, some of whom pretended to be senile while astutely controlling billions of dollars.

Kate had been wise enough to realize that the stock market often operated with little logic, but the routine chaos he depicted made her glad she didn't keep close track of their own small but select portfolio. Compared to his professional world, hers was a model of orderliness and reason.

When she said as much, Adam laughed. "I thought you were always complaining about how crazy advertising is."

"That's true. It's an article of faith on any campaign that if something can go wrong, it will. We just work around that and hope for the best."

"That's exactly how the market operates. Some days I hardly dare to uncross my fingers."

"But you seem to love it."

"I do. The pace either keeps you fueled or burns you out. A lot of guys my age have already gone as far as they can. They're washed up in their mid-thirties because they should never have been on the Street in the first place. But I figure to be around for a long time yet, even if the Dow suddenly decides to run sideways."

Kate believed him. From the first moment they'd met, she had recognized in Adam a fierce determination to meet the world on its own terms and come out on top. It wasn't enough for him simply to succeed; he insisted on having a good time doing it. Perhaps because his early years had been so grim, he had the rare ability to genuinely treasure every day. Now that she had faced up to it, it seemed only natural that he would want to share the fruits of his success

## Gilded Spring

with a child of his own.

They were both quiet most of the way home. Kate stared out the bus window, noticing the large number of men and women pushing strollers. She had read about the upsurge in the birth rate among people in their age group who felt they had postponed childrearing long enough. But not until she had begun to think of becoming part of that trend herself had she noticed how widespread it was. If all those bright young professionals could have babies, why shouldn't she and Adam?

Back home, she showered and slipped into a silk caftan while Adam put together a light supper. It had turned cool, so they made a fire and ate in the living room, sitting cross-legged in front of the fire. Not until they were sipping the last of the wine did Kate work up the courage to interrupt the comfortable silence between them.

Softly she said, "Adam . . . I think it's time we had that talk. All yesterday evening when we were at Carol and Ray's, and then again today in the park, I found myself thinking about having a baby. The more I consider it, the more I like the idea. Oh, I'm not saying I don't have any doubts. The lousy example my own parents set would be enough to give me second thoughts, even without all the added issues of how it would affect our marriage and my career." Her gaze touched his tenderly. "What it comes down to is that I'd really like us to create a child of our own to love and look after together."

A muscle twitched in his jaw as he stared at her intently. "Are you sure you've thought it over enough?"

Kate nodded firmly. "It seems as though I've been

thinking about it for some time without being consciously aware that I was doing so. Does that make any sense?"

"I think I know what you mean. But I want to make sure you're not suggesting this just because you feel it's something I want."

"Do you?"

Adam didn't answer at once. Instead he put both their glasses down on the floor and drew her into his arms. For a long moment he did nothing but hold her. She could feel his heart beating under her cheek and smell the faintly spicy scent of his smooth, cool skin. When his mouth slipped down along the line of her cheek into the sensitive hollow behind her ear, she didn't move. Sitting absolutely still, she let her husband's hands and lips wander over her, savoring the unmistakable sense of being cherished. There was no demand in his touch, only a desire to express how deeply he felt about what was happening between them.

"Yes," he said finally, "I do want a child. I guess I've been going through the same process you have. If anyone had asked me if I'd been thinking about having a baby, I'd probably have said no. But somehow it's crept up on me. Quite unexpectedly, I find that I want it very much."

"That's the way it is with me too." She glanced up at him teasingly. "Must be something to do with hormones—a biological clock..."

Adam laughed, and his arms tightened around her. But his expression was serious as he asked, "Have you considered all the ramifications? Your career, all the things you want to do?"

## Gilded Spring 39

"I haven't made a list of the pluses and minuses. But I don't see any reason why I couldn't have a child and still work. Lots of people do it. We'll be able to afford child care, and I have good maternity benefits." She shrugged as though recognizing that the subject was at once too complex and too basic to be adequately reduced to words.

"You're not scared of it, then?"

"A little," Kate admitted. She smiled weakly. "It's a scary subject. But I imagine a certain degree of apprehension is normal."

He nodded, apparently satisfied that she wasn't being impulsive or underestimating the magnitude of such a decision. His lips brushed hers as he said, "There's something I want to tell you before this goes any further."

Kate stiffened, wondering what on earth might be on his mind. The tension drained from her abruptly as he said, "I think you'd be a fantastic mother. There's no one else I'd ever want to have my children. I can't really express how"—he broke off to search for the right word—"how immensely grateful I am to you for being willing to do this."

There were tears in Kate's eyes as she reached up to stroke his cheek tenderly. Her voice shook slightly as she told him, "I'm not making some gigantic sacrifice, Adam. I want to have a child with you, and I think it's wonderful that you agree."

"We do seem to be on the same wavelength," he said more lightly. For a long moment he continued to stare at her. Then everything seemed to fall into place within his own mind. Bending slightly, he lifted her into his arms and headed for the stairs.

"The dishes..." she murmured weakly.

Against her mouth he said, "Tomorrow."

The curtains in the bedroom were already drawn. Adam set her down, switched on the lamp, then pulled her back into his arms and kissed her very thoroughly. Kate was breathless when he finally lifted his head to look solemnly down at her. "I'll be right back."

Alone, she went over to the dresser. The container holding her diaphragm was in the top drawer. When Adam returned, she was standing there looking at it. He set down the two snifters of cognac he'd brought up with him and went over to her. Studying her closely, he asked, "Any second thoughts?"

Kate shook her head. Her eyes didn't leave Adam's as she tossed the container into the waste basket.

His hands moved caressingly to slip the caftan from her shoulders. Her skin, bared to his gaze, gleamed. With slow deliberation he bent his head to kiss first one rounded breast and then the other. When both nipples were hard and taut, he murmured: "If we have a baby, will you nurse it?"

Kate swallowed, a pulse hammering in her throat. "I—I guess so—for a while..."

He smiled, sensual fires burning in his crystal blue eyes. He pushed the robe completely off Kate and allowed it to fall in a heap on the floor. Her fingers tangled in his crisp dark curls as he continued tantalizing her breasts. A moan broke from her. Frantically she tugged on his hair as he laughed low in his throat.

His powerful arms swung her up. He crossed the room in rapid strides and settled her on the bed. After joining her there, he handed her one of the snifters of

## Gilded Spring 41

cognac. Over the amber liquid, they grinned at each other like fellow conspirators. "To us," Adam said, clinking glasses. "And—whoever."

The taste of the fiery liquid was still on his mouth and hers as they came hungrily together. Their arms and legs entwined, they strained toward each other. His clothes dropped away quickly, forgotten beside the bed.

"God, how I love you!" Adam said with a groan. His mouth followed the path from the cleft between her breasts down her satiny skin to the honeyed nest between her thighs.

A primeval rhythm surged through her. Slowly, carefully, she was being prepared for an act as old as humanity and as enthralling as life itself. For the first time she felt she truly understood its significance.

Adam had always been a patient, generous lover. But now he outdid himself. With seemingly infinite control he brought her closer and closer to the edge of fulfillment until she writhed under him, gasping at rapture so exquisite as to be almost painful. When he gently spread her legs and moved to enter her, she received him with unrestrained delight. Together they rode wave after wave of ecstasy, cresting at a peak higher than either had ever experienced before.

Clinging to each other, trembling with the aftershocks of fulfillment, they descended slowly. Kate's face was wet with her own tears. Adam brushed them away tenderly, not needing to be told she had wept from the sheer beauty of what they had shared.

Kate nestled against him and closed her eyes. Utterly relaxed and at peace, she was almost asleep when some utterly feminine impulse made her whisper, "You know, odds are I won't get pregnant this time."

Against her breasts, Adam smiled. "Then we'll just have to keep at it, won't we," he murmured contentedly.

Convinced that the world could never possibly be better than it was right then, Kate snuggled closer. She did not take another breath before drifting away into dreamless sleep.

## 4

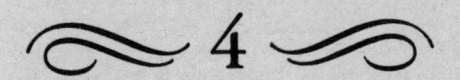

"KATE—IS SOMETHING WRONG?" Adam asked groggily. It was barely dawn several weeks later. He was only half awake but still aware that she was leaving the warm bed.

"Go back to sleep, Adam. Everything's fine."

"How come you're getting up so early?"

"Never mind. Just go back to sleep."

Her matter-of-fact tone combined with his own weariness convinced him to do as she said. Kate breathed a sigh of relief. She felt silly enough without trying to explain why she was awake and out of bed before dawn.

Carefully closing the bathroom door behind her, she switched on the light and read through the instruction booklet again.

"A positive result is indicated by a doughnut shaped ring," it explained. "Results may be visible within forty-five minutes, but for maximum accuracy, wait two hours."

Two hours. If she were sensible, she would go back to sleep. She thought longingly of bed, but knew there was no way she could forget what was taking place in the small plastic vial set on the bathroom counter. Not now that she knew home pregnancy tests were supposed to be extremely accurate, or so the woman at the drugstore had told her.

"How late are you, dear?" she said. "If you don't mind my asking."

"Ten days."

"Oh, well then, this test will definitely work. If you get a positive result, you should plan to see an obstetrician right away."

The woman had smiled as she wrapped up the purchase. Cheerfully she told Kate she had five children of her own and was looking forward to the birth of her first grandchild.

"If you are pregnant, you come back here and we'll fix you up with all your vitamins and the other things you may need."

It had been on the tip of Kate's tongue to ask what other things, but she'd thought better of it. She didn't want to know anything more right then about the potential discomforts of a pregnancy that might or might not exist.

The kitchen was shadowed by the soft gray light of predawn. It was so quiet that the ticking of the wall clock seemed strident. She glanced at it unwillingly. Only five minutes had passed. Sighing, she started a pot of coffee before digging the Femme files out of her briefcase.

The first creative meeting for the account was only a few days off, and so far she had given it little more than cursory thought. That wasn't like her. Much of her professional success was built on meticulous preparation and attention to detail. She could honestly say that she had known every other account she had worked

## Gilded Spring     45

on inside and out. But not this time. As she skimmed the projected budgets, test market analyses, product rationale, and other printed information, she realized how much she still had to learn.

The cosmetics market was intensely competitive. No company would even consider launching a new line without a detailed consideration of the kind of customers they wanted to attract and how best to differentiate their products from the multitude already crowding the shelves.

Femme was no exception. Extensive surveys had shown that the intended market of career women in the twenty-five–to–forty-five age group was both concerned enough about their appearance to want the line and affluent enough to pay the rather steep prices.

So far so good. Now it was Kate's job to make sure Femme's advertising aroused the interest of its potential consumers by appealing to both the practical and romantic sides of women. That was a task she had performed many times before with great success. But at five-thirty in the morning, sitting alone in her kitchen with her mind definitely on other things, she was hard pressed to know where to begin.

In the middle of making desultory notes for the campaign, she found herself doodling a baby's smiling face. Dropping the pencil, she glanced at the clock. Another hour to go. But the pamphlet had said she could check sooner.

On tiptoe, she went back upstairs and passed the bed where Adam still slept. She closed the bathroom door behind her before turning on the light. Leaning forward nervously, she steeled herself to see nothing.

Instead there was a hollow ring that looked exactly like the one depicted in the instruction booklet over the words "Positive Result."

She looked away, blinking. When she glanced back, the ring was still there. Through long moments she watched it intently, certain that it would dissolve. Instead it only grew darker and even more clearly defined.

Don't panic. There's probably some perfectly reasonable explanation. Maybe it hasn't had enough time or the test is faulty—or—I'm pregnant.

Her trembling hands moved instinctively to cup her flat abdomen. Was it possible? Could a tiny human being actually be growing inside her? She looked up, meeting her own gaze in the mirror. Her dark brown eyes were wide and luminous. Her full mouth quivered slightly. All her features seemed softened and enriched.

Slowly, tentatively, she let herself believe at least in the possibility. That alone was enough. Euphoria spread through her like a drug. A baby! A son or daughter to be cherished and given every opportunity to know the world for the wide, wonderful place it could be. A part of herself and Adam joined forever in a living testament to their love.

The temptation to tell him was almost irresistible. But even in the midst of her soul-stirring elation, she realized there was a chance that the results might be wrong. If that turned out to be the case, her own disappointment would be keen enough without inflicting it on him as well. Resolutely Kate dropped the test kit in the trash under a pile of tissues. She made a mental note to take her gynecologist's phone number with her to the office in the hope of getting the earliest possible appointment.

As it turned out, there was a cancellation for that very afternoon.

"Dr. Thorpe's three o'clock appointment won't be able to make it," the receptionist explained. "You could come in then if you like."

Kate swallowed hard. She had expected to have to wait at least a few days. But her sensible side insisted it was better to get the examination over with. "That will be fine."

With the appointment confirmed, she settled down to work. Or at least she tried. As a senior copywriter at the agency she had a large office with windows and a door that, when it was shut, was a silent request that her privacy not be disturbed unless absolutely necessary. That wish was respected, and she was able to make some headway on Femme. By working straight through lunch, she got a basic copy approach outlined before leaving shortly before three o'clock.

At that hour it wasn't hard to get a taxi. She made the trip uptown in twenty minutes while listening to the driver's complaints about the city government, out-of-state drivers, pedestrians, and the ubiquitous pigeons, which, he claimed, made his car a favorite target.

Dr. Thorpe saw Kate with her usual promptness and listened carefully as she described the results of the test she had done that morning. "I wasn't sure how seriously to take it, but—"

"Oh, the test is quite accurate. I don't think I've encountered more than one or two incidents of false results out of thousands."

Kate's eyes widened slightly. "Then it's almost definite that I'm pregnant?"

"I would say so. But let's take a look to make sure."

Back in the examining room she had occupied only a few weeks before, Kate struggled to contain her impatience. When the examination was over, she sat up anxiously. "Am I—?"

Dr. Thorpe grinned. "You certainly are. And everything seems to be fine. After you're dressed, come into my office and we'll chat."

With shaking hands Kate pulled on her clothes and made a vague effort to tidy her hair. Her feet seemed hardly to touch the ground as she walked down the corridor.

The doctor glanced up from the chart she was scribbling on. "Sit down. Unless I miss my guess, that sound I hear is your knees knocking together."

Kate collapsed gratefully in the chair. "I suppose it's silly. After all, I did want to get pregnant. But now that I know it's actually happened, I'm terrified."

"That's perfectly normal. I've had patients who wanted very much to have children but who burst into tears when I told them. Believe me, you'll get used to it."

"How long—I mean, when do you think I'll deliver?"

After consulting a chart the doctor gave her an approximate date. "But don't plan to be too far from home starting about two weeks before then," she warned, "and don't be surprised if the baby isn't born until two weeks afterward. With first pregnancies in particular it's very hard to pinpoint arrival times."

## Gilded Spring     49

Sliding several pamphlets across the desk, she went on. "It would be a good idea to read these. They'll answer some of your questions and probably make you think of more. If anything bothers or frightens you, don't hesitate to call me. It doesn't matter if it's late at night or on the weekend. One of the worst things an expectant mother can do is sit around and worry. I can allay many concerns you may have over the phone and can help a lot of physical problems just as easily."

She went on to list the vitamins Kate should take, explain the importance of a good diet, and add a few admonitions about not overdoing. "Generally speaking, you can continue to follow your usual routine as far as work, excercise, marital relations, and so on are concerned. If you need to slow down, your body will tell you. The best advice I can give is to listen to it."

By the time Kate bundled up all her booklets, sample vitamins, visit schedule, and a folder about natural childbirth, she had been in the office for more than an hour. Yet when she walked out, blinking in the late afternoon sunlight, it felt as though far more time had passed. The difference between suspecting she might be pregnant and knowing for sure was profound.

A faintly giddy smile seemed to have taken up permanent residence on her face. There was a new buoyancy to her step, and she felt a new awareness of her body. The caressingly warm spring air seemed meant especially for her, and the golden sunlight bathing the city gave everything a special glow.

All Kate's senses were gloriously alive. She reveled in the sight of people hurrying home, feeling a lighthearted fondness for each and every one of them. The trees bursting into bud delighted her, as did the clusters of daffodils and crocuses that had dared to poke their heads up into the city air.

A policeman directing traffic at an intersection received a warm grin from her which momentarily startled him before he returned it in full. Kate walked on, humming softly, not minding that she might look a little crazy to some people. She hugged her happiness to herself, savoring all the good things that lay ahead. After she told Adam, she supposed they would call Sherri and Adam's brother. Then there were friends they would want to tell: Carol and Ray, of course, and a few others.

The matter of clothes drifted pleasantly into her thoughts. She had never much liked shopping, but she could hardly wait to look at maternity fashions. With the new, elegant styles she had heard about, she intended to be the best-dressed pregnant woman ever.

Passing a bookstore, she darted in and was astonished to discover that the section on child care was almost as big as the one on careers. Three titles caught her eye. She bought a guide to exercising during pregnancy, an introduction to fatherhood, and a reassuring book about making love while expecting.

She made one more stop before hurrying home, arriving well before Adam was due. After dropping her purchases on the bed, she ran a bath while stripping off her clothes. Jasmine-scented water lapped at her skin as she scrubbed herself all over with a loofah before lying back to soak awhile.

Mindful of the passing time, she didn't linger in

## Gilded Spring

the tub as long as she would have liked. Before the water grew tepid, she dried off and slid into pleated hostess pajamas whose clinging fit and low-cut top would prevent her from ever wearing them in public.

After freshening her makeup and adding a lusty spray of perfume, she tumbled her honey blond hair around her shoulders and hurried downstairs. As she prepared beef stroganoff, patted lettuce dry for a salad, and set the table with the good china and candles, she counted the moments until Adam would be home.

By the time she heard his key in the door, she was ready. Meeting him in the hallway, she brushed a kiss against his lean cheek as his arms closed around her.

"Hmmm, you smell good," he murmured. Setting her back a bit, he let his eyes wander appreciatively over her. "I haven't seen that outfit before, have I?"

"Nope, it's new. How was your day?"

"Fine. More stocks went up than down. How about you?"

"Pretty good. I'm making some progress on Femme. Would you like a drink before dinner?"

Adam frowned slightly. Her cheeks were flushed, and she was talking fast, as though she was somehow nervous. His frown deepened as he remembered that she had seemed a little off stride that morning. And she had gotten up so early.

Very gently he said, "Sweetheart, is something bothering you?"

Kate bit her lip. She didn't want to spoil her surprise by blurting it out, but she should have realized he would sense some change in her. Determined to distract him, she teased, "Yes, you are. You're not allowed to look so serious on such a beautiful spring day. Come into the kitchen and put your feet up while I make you a drink."

He went along without objection, tossing his jacket on a chair and unfastening his tie without taking his attention from her. Beneath the thin burgundy silk she wore, her back was very straight and her shoulders seemed tense. Not even the delectable curve of her bottom, clearly visible through the fragile material, could distract him from the growing conviction that something strange was going on.

He was about to try once more to find out what it might be when the sight of the dining room table gleaming under a full complement of crystal, silver, and china drew him up short. Confident that he had not overlooked an anniversary, birthday, or observance of any other kind, he asked, "What's the occasion?"

"Oh—I just thought it wouldn't do us any harm to put on the dog a bit."

Adam didn't buy that. Kate was not the sort of compulsive woman who rushed home from the office to prepare an elaborate meal, drag out formal place settings they didn't use more than once or twice a year, and slip into a decidedly slinky outfit unless she had a very good reason.

Coming up behind her at the counter, he set his hands down on either side of her, neatly trapping her in place. "Okay," he said, "suppose you tell me what this is all about."

Kate turned within the circle of his arms and smiled up at him. "Guess."

"You got a promotion?"

"Nope. Try again."

"You won the lottery?"

"Not as far as I know. Give up?"

When he nodded, she laughed softly. "I bought you a present."

Puzzlement clouded Adam's blue eyes. "All this for a present?"

"You haven't seen it yet."

Before he could react, she slipped under his arm and picked up a gaily wrapped package on the kitchen table. "Here. Maybe you should open it now."

Looking from her to the package and back again, Adam complied. He made short work of the wrapping and held up a beautifully made scale replica of a locomotive engine.

"Oh—it's terrific! I've always wanted to start a train collection. But why—?"

"Remember *when* you were going to start it?"

"When? I don't understand..." The words trailed away as he stared at her, open-mouthed.

His stunned expression brought a chuckle of pure glee from Kate. For years it had been a running joke between them that he would finally get his long-desired train set when they had a baby.

Adam took a deep breath, struggling to contain the surge of excitement darting through him. "You mean—?" Smiling widely, she nodded.

In the next instant she was in his arms, held with such reverent tenderness that her throat tightened. She could feel his big body trembling against her as he whispered, "Oh, Kate...my beautiful Kate...no man could ever be happier than you've made me."

The husky timbre of his voice and the undisguised

vulnerability of his emotions moved her deeply. Feeling infinitely cherished, she nestled closer to him. For long, precious moments the outside world with all its multitude of problems faded away. There was only Adam and the joy of having his child growing inside her.

## 5

"You two don't waste any time once you make up your minds to do something, do you?" Carol teased.

Ray laughed indulgently, raising his glass to Adam in salute. "I always knew you were efficient, buddy. Here's to another job well done."

"Hey, don't I get any credit?" Kate demanded good-naturedly. "After all, I'm involved in this project too."

They were all seated in the Remington's living room after enjoying the dinner Kate and Adam had prepared together. A bottle of champagne stood open in an ice bucket, but only the men were drinking it. After a couple of token sips, the women had switched to lemonade.

Carol patted her rounding stomach contentedly as she told Kate, "Of course you're involved. You'll be fussed over until you're sick of it. Hasn't that started yet?"

Kate nodded ruefully and laughed at Adam's chagrined expression. Ever since he had learned of his impending fatherhood, he had barely allowed her to lift a finger. Whereas before they had always shared the usual weekend chores of shopping, laundry, cleaning, and so on, now he insisted on doing everything himself.

Only with great difficulty had she managed to convince him not to drive her to work each morning. They had compromised, with Kate agreeing to call him as soon as she reached her office. Unless he was absolutely swamped, he managed to phone at least once during the day to check on her. His solicitude meant a great deal to her, though she couldn't help but find it a bit funny.

Carol didn't need to have the situation spelled out for her. Glancing from Kate to Adam, sitting close together on the couch, she told Kate, "Don't worry, husbands calm down after the first few months. They don't start really worrying again until the last few weeks."

"Not me," Ray claimed. "This time, I'm cool as a cucumber."

Carol grinned. "The cucumber was up in the middle of the night watching me sleep. He said I wasn't breathing often enough."

Caught in the middle of swallowing the last of his champagne, Adam sputtered as it went down the wrong way. Everyone laughed. "That makes me feel better," he finally admitted. "I keep staring at Kate, thinking she ought to look different. But she doesn't."

"Give her time," Carol advised kindly. "By Christmas you'll think you're living with a blimp."

"I still can hardly believe it," Kate said, looking down at herself. "I keep wondering how I'll ever get big enough to make room for the baby."

"Oh, don't worry about that," Carol assured her. "Nature has a marvelous way of taking care of it. Just be careful to eat properly and drink plenty of water, because your body is busy making all sorts of new things."

"She will," Adam said so firmly that both women chuckled. Unabashedly he added, "I consider this very much a team effort from start to finish. Kate's certainly got the hardest part, but at least I can help."

"Does that mean you're planning on natural childbirth?" Ray asked.

Kate nodded quickly. "Of course. These days, is there any other way?"

Carol hesitated a moment before she said, "If you wouldn't mind a piece of advice, it's a good idea not to be too rigid about that. As we told you, Ray and I had a wonderful experience with Davey's birth. But it was a very close call with us. I was in labor almost as long as my doctor felt was safe. I'm thrilled that it worked out the way it did, but frankly, in another hour or so I would have agreed to a cesarean."

Adam's arm resting on Kate's shoulders tightened protectively. "To be honest," he said, "I have mixed feelings about natural childbirth. I definitely want to be there and see our baby being born, but I can't stand the idea of Kate being in pain."

Carol's eyes were gently compassionate as she said, "Having a baby hurts, Adam. There's no way around that. The doctor can safely give some anesthetics, but it's best to administer as little as possible."

Kate saw that Adam looked deeply concerned.

"All I'm saying," Carol went on, "is that a woman shouldn't make completely natural childbirth a rigid goal, so that if she does end up needing help, she feels as though she has somehow failed. Nothing really matters except that the mother and baby come through fine. Anything else, wonderful though it may be, is extraneous."

Ray agreed completely. "After seeing Davey born, I want very much to be there for our new baby's arrival. But not if that means Carol has to go through a moment's more pain just to make it possible. If that were the case, I'd rather be out in the waiting room pacing back and forth like in those old cartoons we used to see."

"I may join you," Adam muttered, grimly considering the more unpleasant aspects of childbirth. Kate was young and healthy and the doctor said everything was going well, but it was early days yet. Who knew what the next few months might bring. As much as he wanted a child, the thought of her suffering tormented him.

Seeing his distress, Kate determinedly changed the subject. They talked about plans for the annual block party, the upcoming primary elections, in which their congressional district representation was being contested, and the efforts to get more frequent trash pickup despite cuts in the city's services budget.

As the evening passed, Kate was struck by the feeling that her and Adam's friendship with Carol and Ray, which had always been strong, was now on firmer ground than ever. Their shared involvement in childbearing had brought them even closer. It was good to know she would be able to turn to Carol for advice and guidance as her pregnancy progressed, and she suspected Adam would do the same with Ray.

Ruefully she admitted that another good reason for being friends with a couple going through the same experience was that they were just as disinclined to stay up late. Well before midnight, the men were in the kitchen finishing off the dishes while the women chatted quietly in the living room.

"Have you told Sherri and Bill yet?" Carol asked.

"We called them yesterday." Kate smiled, remembering her sister and brother-in-law's delight. Though they were parents three times over themselves, there was no mistaking their pleasure in the news that they would soon have a niece or nephew to spoil.

"I hope Adam is keeping an eye on you," Sherri had admonished. "You know you have a tendency to overdo."

"He's practically sitting on me," Kate assured her. "I promise, everything is fine. I feel great, and I couldn't be happier."

"That's how it should be," Bill interrupted. She could picture them standing close to each other in the homey kitchen, his bronzed arm draped around Sherri's slender waist. After ten years of marriage, they were more in love than ever. All the problems they had faced raising three children and keeping the winery going had only strengthened the bond between them.

When Kate contrasted the deeply rooted strength of Sherri and Bill with the superficial relationships of people like her parents, she was even more grateful for all she shared with Adam. Purely by coincidence, both her mother and father had happened to be at their luxurious Palm Beach retirement home when she had called. They had greeted the news of Kate's pregnancy as cordially as if she had announced that she had won a game of tennis. When the baby was born, they would undoubtedly send a large check. The next time one or both of them were in New York, they might stop by to visit. But they were too self-centered to think of giving more.

Even after years of coping with their disinterest, Kate wasn't immune to the pain it caused. But she was determined not to let it get to her. She already had more than enough to cope with. Being pregnant, she found, had some surprising ramifications. She was just beginning to understand that it was in many ways the ultimate expression not only of her love for Adam but also of the absolute trust she had in him. She knew she could count on him totally to stand by her through an experience that, despite all the joy, was more than a little frightening.

"Sherri and Bill are thrilled," she told Carol softly. "So is Adam's brother. The thought of being an uncle has sent Brandon over the moon."

She didn't add that her brother-in-law's enthusiasm had surprised her. Brandon was two years younger than Adam and claimed to be a confirmed bachelor. He too had fought his way out of the Appalachian coal fields to become a successful corporate lawyer in San Francisco. Though the brothers rarely saw each other, they kept in close touch. The early deaths of their parents had led them to look out for each other.

When Adam had first announced that he and Kate were getting married, Brandon had flown all the way to New York to look her over and make sure his brother wasn't making a mistake. Far from being offended, Kate had liked him at once simply because he cared so much for Adam. Over the years she had found many more reasons to appreciate her brother-in-law. When he had promised to come east again after the baby was born, she'd been delighted.

"Most people are glad to hear a baby is on the way," Carol commented. Teasingly she added, "Especially when they know they aren't going to be the ones changing the diapers and walking the floor at night."

"I won't be surprised if Adam insists on doing most of that. He's determined to be involved every step of the way." Kate laughed softly. "I think if I had morning sickness, he'd even want to share that."

"I take it that means you haven't had any yet?"

"Not a twinge," Kate said proudly. "None of the fatigue I've heard about, either. Maybe I'll be lucky and breeze through this."

"Maybe you will, but try to make allowances in case it doesn't work out that way."

"If I were going to be sick, wouldn't it have already started?"

"Not necessarily. You're only a few weeks along. Your body may not begin to feel the strain until you've gone a couple of months." Reassuringly she added, "But even if you do start feeling worn out and nauseous, it doesn't usually last very long. Most of us seem to adjust very quickly."

Kate didn't think that sounded too bad. Feeling a little ill in the mornings and getting tired more easily than usual was a small price to pay for a child. Maybe she'd work at home one or two days, and it might be a good idea to get more sleep. But there didn't seem to be anything she couldn't handle.

Nevertheless, when Carol and Ray left a short time later, she was feeling unusually tired. Adam finished tidying up while she cleaned her face and slipped into a nightgown. By the time he joined her, she was stretched out in bed, looking through one of the pamphlets Dr. Thorpe had given her.

"I started reading that book on being a father," Adam said as he undressed. "It's full of information I didn't know."

"No kidding?" Kate murmured airily. "I thought maybe you had half a dozen kids squirreled away somewhere."

"Cute." Naked, he walked over to the bed and stood staring down at her. "How are you feeling? A few minutes ago you looked worn out."

"I was," she admitted. "But I just needed to lie down. I'm fine now." She put the pamphlet on the bedside table and pulled back the blanket. "If you slip that gorgeous body in here, I'll show you just how good I am."

Adam laughed, but when he joined her under the covers, he did no more than take her gently in his arms. Kate enjoyed his tender embrace, but she was in the mood for far more. So was Adam, as his unmistakable state of arousal told her. Yet he made no move to initiate lovemaking, nor did he respond to her own tentative caresses.

Finally she was forced to ask, "Adam... what you said downstairs—about not being able to stand the idea of me being in pain—was that true?"

He shifted slightly to look at her in the dim light filtering through the drawn curtains. "Of course it was. The only negative aspect I can see to our having a baby is what you're going to go through."

Against the smooth, cool skin of his chest, she

smiled. "I'm not exactly fragile, you know."

She felt his muscles tighten. "I realize that. But you're not invulnerable, either. I'm—afraid of your being hurt."

Very gently Kate reached up to stroke the hard line of his jaw. "Is that why we haven't made love since I told you about the baby? Because you're afraid of hurting me?"

He let out a deep sigh. Glumly he nodded. "I guess so. You know we tend to—get carried away, and I worry about doing something that might cause problems."

"Haven't you read the part in the book about intercourse being perfectly safe?"

"Yes," he admitted. "But reading it and believing it are two different things."

"Maybe the solution is just to *do* it."

He looked doubtfully at her. "I don't want you to feel obligated in any way."

"Adam, for heaven's sake! In case you haven't noticed these last five years, I happen to enjoy making love with you. If I can't persuade you there's no danger, I'll be a crazy lady by the time the baby is born."

His utterly male growl of amusement convinced her he was willing to be swayed. Turning over so that she was beneath him, he muttered, "You're already crazy. And I love every nutty inch of you."

Her brown eyes gleamed provocatively. "Then prove it."

Adam stared at her for a long moment before he accepted the challenge. Holding his weight off her, he tenderly brushed stray wisps of hair from her forehead before slowly following the line of her smooth brow down along her upturned nose to her full mouth.

When his lips followed the same path, Kate moaned softly. She was on fire with need for him, but Adam would not be hurried. Drawing out every caress to the utmost, he made absolutely sure she would be able to receive him.

His tongue flicked out to taste the silken hollow at the base of her throat before circling all the way around the full curve of her breasts. Thickly he muttered, "Are they tender?"

"A little."

"If I hurt you, tell me."

Cupping the swollen globes, she raised them to him in offering. "You won't. Please..."

When his mouth gently took her nipple, she arched against him. Over and over he alternately licked and suckled the taut peak until it seemed impossible for her to bear any more. When his dark head moved to work the same magic on her other breast, she tried to stop him. But he refused to be deterred. Gently but determinedly he brought her to a pinnacle of desire so intense that waves of yearning crashed through her.

A low whimper broke from her as he slid down the silken length of her body, his hands gently squeezing her breasts as his knee urged her legs apart. As her most sensitive flesh was bathed in exquisite pleasure, she writhed under him. Helplessly, she tangled her fingers in his thick hair.

"A-Adam...no more...please..."

Hesitantly he straightened above her. The crystal fire in his eyes made her throat tighen. Tautly he demanded, "Are you sure?"

# Gilded Spring

Kate was beyond speech. She could only nod as her hands stroked down the hard line of his chest, along his narrow hips, to tell him as clearly as possible what she wanted.

Still Adam held back. His desperate need warred with a deep uncertainty. If he were to hurt her...

It was left to Kate to solve their problem. Gently she urged him onto his back. Realizing what she intended, Adam complied quickly. Stretched out beneath her, he gave himself up to her care.

Balanced on her knees, Kate bent her lips to his, slipping her tongue into his mouth at the same time that she brought them carefully together. At first she touched only the hot, pulsing tip of him, building his arousal and her own until the need to have all of him became irresistible. As her body sank completely around his, Adam groaned deep in his throat.

"What you do to me!"

Kate laughed softly, a purely womanly sound that rippled on the cool night air. Then the laughter dissolved into moans of pleasure as Adam began to thrust carefully within her. Dimly she registered the feeling that he seemed even bigger than usual. The sensation was exquisitely overpowering, driving her to arch against him at every stroke.

She was turning to liquid inside, her consciousness vanishing into a fiery mist. Adam waited just until she reached fulfillment before releasing himself, her name breaking from him as undulating waves of pleasure hurled them both to the furthest reaches of ecstasy.

# 6

"I THINK YOU'RE really onto something with your outline for the Femme campaign," Lois Hardesty said. "This idea that women can get ahead in the world without sacrificing their femininity just might fly."

"Thanks," Kate murmured a bit weakly. Lois's opinion meant a great deal to her, not simply because she was her boss at the agency but because she was also one of the most experienced and astute copywriters anywhere. In her mid-forties, having made the long, hard climb up the career ladder in the days before women's lib, Lois was renowned for being able to spot new market trends and make the most of them. If she said the campaign was solid, chances were it would be a big hit.

Knowing that, Kate wondered why she didn't feel more enthusiastic. Maybe the fact that she was having trouble keeping her eyes open had something to do with it. Despite having gotten ten hours of sleep, she had barely been able to crawl out of bed that morning. Adam had had to coax her into the shower and then practically help her dress. After he left her on the bus, she had dozed off again and almost missed her stop.

Now, barely managing to stifle a yawn, she struggled to listen to what Lois was saying. "This concept should work equally well in print ads and on TV. I'd like you to start developing rough copy and layouts for the ads we talked about at the planning meeting, and then give some thought to a story board for a thirty-second commercial."

"Oh, sure... I'll get started right away." As soon as I stop feeling as though I'm going to lose the breakfast I didn't even eat.

Lois's gaze shifted from the notes she held in her hand to Kate's strained face. Her voice dropped slightly, becoming more gentle. "Hey, are you all right?"

Kate hesitated. She wasn't absolutely sure how her boss was going to react to the news that she was pregnant. Carefully she said, "I've felt better."

"Maybe you've picked up that virus that's making the rounds. Two guys in the art department are out with it."

"Uh—no—I don't think that's it."

Lois's smooth brow rose beneath her carefully coiffed auburn hair. "Kate, you know I don't intrude on the personal lives of my staff, but if there's anything you want to talk about..."

Touched by the offer of a sympathetic ear, Kate regetted her earlier hesitation. Lois was too warm-hearted and intelligent a woman not to understand that just because she had never attempted to combine a career and motherhood didn't mean other women couldn't successfully do so. Smiling a bit shyly, she said, "I'm pregnant."

The look of blank astonishment on the copy chief's normally composed features made Kate laugh. She had finally managed to shock Lois Hardesty!

## Gilded Spring 69

"Good lord!" the older woman murmured when she was at last able to respond. Her expression became thoughtful as her eyes settled on Kate's face. "You are, aren't you? I should have realized."

It was Kate's turn to look surprised. "You couldn't have known. I only found out a week ago myself."

"Yes, but you're different. Quiet; a little withdrawn. Even more so than when you're locked in a creative burst. And there's a certain glow..." Lois laughed softly. "You may not feel at your best, but you certainly look it. It must be true what people say about pregnant women always being beautiful."

"Believe me, I feel anything but beautiful! I was so proud of myself for not having any unpleasant symptoms, and now—"

"Now you have to concentrate to hold your head up?"

"That's about the size of it. But I'm sure I'll snap out of it."

"Of course you will," Lois reassured her. "Why, I remember when my sister was pregnant with her first..." She went on reminiscing about the birth of her eldest niece as Kate listened in growing amazement. Her boss had never spoken of her family before, had certainly never revealed what was clearly her deep love for them all.

"So you really have to expect not to feel all that well," Lois concluded. "We may have to make some adjustment in your work schedule. But don't worry about that. We'll deal with it if and when it's necessary."

Though she had hoped for some support and understanding when her pregnancy became known, Kate was frankly amazed by her boss's calm acceptance of the situation. When she said as much, Lois looked at her very seriously.

"You're a highly valued member of my staff, Kate. I'm well aware that you could walk out of here and get a job with another agency immediately, or decide to free-lance. I'm not about to do anything to encourage that. Besides, I happen to think it's important for people like you and Adam to have children. You have a great deal to contribute to the next generation. In the long run we all benefit."

Lois's words took Kate back a bit. She really had not considered that what she was doing might be of use to the human race. Neither was she convinced that Lois thought in such grandiose terms. But the older woman was able to look beyond the immediate problems her condition might cause and consider the larger picture. For that Kate was grateful even as she clung to the conviction that she would be feeling like her old self in no time.

By afternoon Kate was beginning to wonder if she might not be wrong about that. She was so tired that she could no longer ignore it. Every bone and muscle in her body ached. Her stomach had stopped churning, but the mere thought of food started her head reeling again. At lunchtime she barely managed to swallow part of a Coke while worrying about whether the lack of nutritious food might be harming the baby. Was it lying inside her wondering when a decent meal would arrive?

That bit of whimsy wrung a smile from her. Glancing down at her flat tummy, she murmured, "Don't

## Gilded Spring

worry. If worse comes to worse, you can call out for pizza."

"Who are you talking to?"

She looked up to find Pete, the secretary who worked for her and two other copywriters, standing in the doorway. A dropout from the back rows of the City Ballet corps, he had the rare qualitites of tolerance, good humor, and tirelessness. More than once he had helped keep Kate sane in the midst of chaos. Apparently he thought another such effort was called for.

"I know this place can get to you," Pete said gravely, "but carrying on conversations with your stomach is a little weird even for around here."

"I don't know about that. It depends on what kind of answer you get."

Flopping down in the chair across from Kate's desk, he rolled his eyes worriedly. "So your stomach's coming through with good messages? Well, why don't you tell Dr. Pete all about it?"

"It says," Kate informed him with mock sternness, "that a certain smart-ass secretary had better watch himself."

"It's more fun to watch you. How often do I get a chance to see a big deal copywriter going around the bend?"

"Every day, I would imagine. You know we pride ourselves on not being too tightly wired." With a touch of smugness she added, "Anyway, it just so happens that you've misinterpreted the entire situation. I was not talking to my stomach."

"Your belly button?"

"No."

"I could go on, but this is a family show. How about clearing up the mystery?"

"I was talking to Willy."

Now Pete really did look worried. It wasn't unheard of for very talented people to develop cracks in the old psyche. Warily he repeated, "Willy?"

"Yep. You'd think a person in my line of work would be able to come up with a more creative name for her baby, wouldn't you? But that's the best I can do right now."

Pete's reaction was even more satisfying than Lois's. He stared wide-eyed for long moments before a huge smile wreathed his face. "Oh, my gosh! That's fantastic!"

"I think it's pretty nice," Kate agreed blandly.

"*Nice!* How can you be so calm about it? Have you told Adam? Silly question. Of course you have. Does Lois know? You realize everyone's going to go nuts when they hear. Nobody at the agency has had a baby in ages. When will it be born? Do we have to wait long?"

By the time he finally paused to breathe, Kate couldn't hold back her laughter. "Good heavens, if I'd known being pregnant would make me so popular, I'd have done it ages ago."

"That's all right," Pete allowed magnanimously. "You've been busy. But I'm delighted you finally got around to it." Sitting back, he grinned widely. "A baby. A little copywriter."

"God forbid!"

"Or maybe a miniature art director."

"Never!"

# Gilded Spring 73

"Does that mean you want it to take after Adam?"

"Better that than what you're suggesting."

Pete shrugged tolerantly. "Oh, all right. Just so long as we all get to see it and play with it." Leaning forward slightly, he called, "Hi in there, Willy. Uncle Pete here. How's it going?"

"You're crazier than I am."

"It's very important to talk to babies," he insisted. "Who knows when they actually start learning." Nodding firmly, he added, "I'll buy a book. That way I'll be able to keep track of what's happening month to month."

"You already have me organized within an inch of my life. Now you want to do the same thing to a defenseless baby?"

"Absolutely. If I leave everything to you, you'll probably forget you're supposed to be helping Willy grow ears one week and work on toes the next."

He spoke with such seriousness that Kate had to bite back the urge to laugh. "It's all instinctive," she protested weakly.

The look he shot her was an unmistakable reprimand. "That's no excuse for turning in a slipshod performance. No, we're going to do this right. To start with, what did you eat today?"

"Oh, lord, not you too? Adam is driving me crazy about that."

"As he should be. Answer the question."

"I had a Coke."

Pete looked truly appalled. It took him a moment to recover enough to say, "You can't do that to Willy."

"It wasn't by choice. I just can't bear even to think of food."

Reproach gave way to sympathy. "Is your tum-tum upset?"

"Pete, I'm having a baby. I haven't turned into one."

"Sorry. Let's try that again. About ready to barf, are you?"

Kate groaned. "I think I preferred tum-tum."

"Never mind. Here's what we'll do. I'll go down to the gourmet shop on the corner and get you some of their very nice vegetable soup and some crackers. You should be able to manage that, don't you think?"

Actually that didn't sound bad at all. Kate wondered why she hadn't thought of it herself. Of course, it seemed to require all her brain cells to remember where she was and what she was supposed to be doing.

"That would be nice... but I can't ask you to—"

"You didn't ask. I offered. Now you just stay right there and I'll be back in a jiff."

True to his word, Pete returned a short time later with a steaming mug of soup and a half dozen crackers which, he was careful to point out, were salt free. When she had finished the meal, Kate had to admit she felt better—at least well enough to get through the rest of the day without dozing off.

Even so, she left a bit early in the hope of missing the worst of the rush-hour traffic, only to discover that an awful lot of other people seemed to have had the same idea. Her bus was jammed. She barely had room to stand, let alone sit down.

The trip seemed endless. Squeezed between an overweight woman who was sweating profusely despite the cool air and an irate businessman who insisted on trying to read a newspaper that kept getting in Kate's face, she had to struggle to breathe.

Very quickly it became apparent that Pete's soup, delicious though it had been, was not doing her any good. By the time she finally reached her stop, her senses were reeling. Stumbling off the bus, she noted vaguely that the sidewalk seemed to ripple in front of her. She gingerly put one foot in front of the other and concentrated all her efforts on getting home before she disgraced herself.

Long, unpleasant moments in the bathroom helped somewhat, but when they were over she felt utterly drained. It was all she could do to reach the bed, where she flopped down, exhausted. Without even the strength to get out of her clothes, she could only lie there motionless until she heard Adam come home.

From the hallway where she knew he was glancing through the mail, he called, "Hi, honey! Gorgeous day, wasn't it?"

Wincing at his cheerfulness, Kate struggled to sit up. Her whole body felt as though it had been used as a punching bag. Though she didn't have a vain bone in her, she wasn't about to let him find her like that. Weaving her way back into the bathroom, she was safely sequestered behind the closed door when he came upstairs.

She could hear him moving around, dropping his briefcase near the bed, taking off his jacket, all the while whistling softly. There was a pause, and she imagined him glancing toward the closed door.

"Kate—is everything all right?"

Summoning the last of her strength, she managed to sound as though she didn't have a care in the world. "Of course. I'll be right out."

That seemed to satisfy him. He sang a few more bars of "Yes, Sir, That's My Baby" before adding, "What do you want to do about dinner tonight?"

Nothing. I never want to see food again as long as I live. From now on I'm living on air.

"Oh, I don't know. What are you in the mood for?"

That was a mistake. She knew it the moment the words were out, but it was too late to stop Adam from replying. "I skipped lunch today, so I'm starved. How about we go down to Romano's and get some of that really great fettuccine with clam sauce?"

Oh no...

"Or maybe we could get takeout from that burger place with the good onions and fries. What do you think?"

He's doing this deliberately. All of a sudden I'm married to a sadist.

"Anything you want will be fine, honey. I may just... skip dinner..."

There was silence, but only for a moment. She heard the firm sound of steps outside the door, followed quickly by, "Kate, if you're not feeling well, you should just say so. After all, it's perfectly normal."

The vague undercurrent of amusement in his voice struck her dumb. He actually thought this was funny! How would he like to hang over the sink while the insides of his body turned to jell-o?

After washing out her mouth, she opened the door a crack and glared at him. "I'm busy. Go away—and take your gross eating habits with you."

Far from being offended, he merely smiled toler-

## Gilded Spring

antly and pushed the door fully open. "Feeling that rotten, huh?"

"No worse than something that's been dead for a week."

Adam smiled indulgently. It was just like her to try to pretend pregnancy wasn't having any impact. He would have to watch her even more carefully. "You should have told me right away that you weren't feeling well. As I mentioned, it's—"

"I know," Kate interrupted, in no mood for solicitude from someone who had the nerve to be in such obvious good health. "It's perfectly normal. Somehow I suspect I'm going to get very tired of hearing that. There is nothing remotely normal about the way I feel."

"Well, then," he murmured benevolently, "I think it would be a good idea for you to get back into bed." Without waiting for her reply, he lifted her firmly and strode across the room.

Having just become more or less accustomed to being vertical, the abrupt separation of her feet from the floor left Kate gasping. "Put me down!"

"In a minute. First I'm going to get you out of these clothes."

"I am perfectly capable of undressing myself."

"Of course you are. Hold still just a sec—that's right, lift your arm—good girl."

Too weary to fight him, even verbally, she had no choice but to let him strip her. When she was completely naked, Adam helped her lie down and tucked the covers firmly around her. Sitting on the side of the bed, he laid a possessive hand on her belly. "You're going to stay right where you are until tomorrow morning, and no arguments. Even someone as stubborn as you should understand that you just can't go right on as though nothing has changed."

"But I'm not sick. I'm only—"

"Pregnant. With child. In a delicate condition. However you want to put it, you have to make allowances for yourself."

Kate felt compelled to point out in her own defense that she had left the office early, but Adam wasn't impressed. "What does that mean? That you ducked out half an hour before the rest of them? You'll have to do better than that. At least for these first few months, when your system is adjusting to the baby."

She supposed he didn't really mean the words as unsympathetically as they sounded. But in the aftermath of a day that had pushed her to the very limits, Kate couldn't help but feel resentful of his presumption that she wasn't making enough concessions to her condition.

"I do still have a job, you know," she pointed out tartly. "Even though Lois was very happy to learn about the baby, I don't think she'd be too thrilled if I suddenly stopped showing up."

Far from seeming to understand her point, Adam merely shrugged. "It doesn't matter what Lois thinks. You have to put yourself and the baby first."

"But my job *is* a big part of me. I can't just walk away from it." Exhaustion made her voice faint, further increasing her impatience with the strange new sensations surging through her.

Neither did Adam help any when he insisted, "That's fine. But I think you need to reassess your priorities.

# Gilded Spring

No job is as important as the baby."

Vaguely Kate tried to tell him there was no reason she couldn't have both. She just needed a little time to adjust, and a little understanding of what drove her to hold on fiercely to her professional identity even as she began for the first time in her life to think of herself as a mother.

But the words wouldn't come. She had no strength left. Her eyelids fluttered for barely an instant before she fell into dreamless sleep.

# 7

"How are you holding up?" Carol asked over the phone. "Everything going all right?"

"Oh, yes," Kate said swiftly. "I saw my doctor again yesterday, and she was very reassuring."

A hint of annoyance in her voice must have alerted her friend to what she was thinking, because Carol laughed softly. "Let me guess. She said something along the lines of, 'I'm sorry, but everything you're feeling is normal and there's nothing I can do about it.' Am I close?"

"Right on target. Do they all learn that in obstetrics school?"

"Could be. It's certainly the standard comment. Trouble is, it's also true. There isn't anything they can do."

"She did say there are pills for morning sickness. But as hard as it is to believe, I don't have it bad enough to risk taking them."

Over the phone line, Carol sighed sympathetically. "It didn't comfort me either to know there were women worse off than me."

"Speaking of which, how are *you* feeling?"

"Oh, I'm fine. Now that I'm through the first

trimester, it should be clear sailing up to the last few weeks."

Hoping Carol was right, Kate asked, "Is Ray doing as well?"

A soft chuckle reached her despite the din of traffic outside her office window. "Not quite. But he's getting there. However, I now have a new watchdog. Ever since Davey found out he has a brother or sister on the way, he hasn't been able to take his eyes off me."

"I'll bet he's got a ton of questions."

"You know it! We're following the policy of answering them all truthfully but not bombarding him with information that might frighten or bewilder him. So far he seems to be coping well."

Kate grinned as she caught herself wondering how she would handle the same situation when the time came. She hadn't even had one child yet and she was already thinking ahead to the next one, despite the fact that she still felt queasy off and on every day and found even the slightest physical effort to be a chore. Shaking her head at the marvels of nature, she promised Carol to stay in touch before going reluctantly back to work.

Since Adam had gotten their old car out of storage and begun driving her back and forth to the office, she had to admit she did have a little more energy. Though she had objected strenuously when he first announced the plan, she no longer had any desire to go back to taking the bus.

In a city where traffic was constantly snarled and parking spots could be more precious than gold, it was almost sinfully luxurious to get around without lifting a finger. Fortunately Adam didn't seem to mind the trip at all. The man who only a few months before had said it was insane to try to drive in New York now did so with determined relish. He even accepted without comment the exorbitant fee he had to pay in order to park near his office each day. It seemed to satisfy some deeply rooted need in him to deposit her safely in front of the McKay agency building each morning and collect her from there each evening.

Several people in the office who had noticed her comings and goings kidded her about them, but Kate didn't mind. Since word of her pregnancy had spread over the office grapevine, she had noticed a definite change in the way her colleagues treated her. Those who already had children were more relaxed and forthcoming, as though she had somehow joined a club whose existence she had never before suspected. Others who might be contemplating taking the parental plunge themselves were frankly curious about how she and Adam had reached the decision and what impact it was having on them so far. Even some with no immediate or even likely prospects of having children found a vicarious excitement and pleasure in knowing a new life was on the way.

If any of them resented her or doubted her ability to continue to do her job, they did not reveal their feelings. They were stopped by Lois's firm support and the knowledge that David McKay wanted his agency to be thought of as an enlightened, family-oriented organization.

"So far, so good, Willy," Kate murmured as she

patted her stomach and decided that from a professional viewpoint at least, things weren't going too badly.

Several hours later she had further confirmation of that when she joined Lois in presenting the preliminary Femme ads to the head of the agency. David McKay's office was on the floor above the copy and art departments. A vast reception area, which seemed to be completely covered in beige ultrasuede, gave way to the offices of account executives clustered as closely as possible around the northwest corner, from which their boss ruled his domain.

At forty-five, David McKay had the silver hair, smooth features, and perpetual tan of the affluent. Kate sensed that it was a source of profound satisfaction to him that his world did not stretch further than the manicured links of private golf courses and the dance floors of society balls. She doubted he had ever known a moment of uncertainty or hardship. Yet for all the narrowness of his personal experience, he had an uncanny sense of what would sell to people far removed from his own way of life.

That coupled with the fact that it was his name that appeared at the bottom of her paychecks made her give close attention to the formalities of securing his approval.

McKay rose from his desk as she and Lois were ushered in by a secretary who combined just the right degree of good looks and starched efficiency. He smiled benignly as the two women took seats around the low-slung glass-and-chrome coffee table.

Lois usually touched base with her boss several times a week, but Kate had not seen him in a couple of months, so it was on her that his attention focused.

"Before we get down to work," he said, "let me congratulate you on your marvelous news. Children are truly a blessing."

Kate accepted his good wishes cordially. One of the few things she did find appealing about McKay was his genuine love for his family. A group picture of his wife, two sons, and daughter was displayed prominently on his desk, and other photos were scattered around the office. Unlike many men in his position, he had a reputation for not taking advantage of the sexual opportunities that were so readily available.

Knowing that, Kate was surprised to realize that his eyes were wandering over her with unmistakably male appreciation. A dull flush warmed her cheeks as she realized she was witnessing a classic case of what she had read about only the previous night— that some men found pregnant women extraordinarily attractive. Far from being repelled by the condition, they were drawn by the unique interaction of sensuality and prohibition. Such looks from Adam delighted her, but the realization that her boss was similarly aroused put her nerves on edge.

All the while McKay listened to the reasons behind the proposed copy, he watched her intently. Kate had to draw on every ounce of her self-control to appear unperturbed by his scrutiny. To her further embarrassment, she quickly realized that Lois was well aware of what was going on.

The copy chief's body language alone was enough to make that clear. Barely minutes into the discussion, she adroitly maneuvered herself so that she was seated between them. Lois did most of the talking and fielded almost all McKay's questions. All Kate had to do was say a few words about her ideas for the final copy version and count the minutes until she could escape.

They couldn't have been in McKay's office more than half an hour, but the time had seemed endless. As they walked back downstairs, Lois shook her head ruefully. "I've never seen the old goat behave like that before. You really threw him."

"He didn't do my equilibrium much good either," Kate replied.

"Oh, well, at least he approved the campaign."

Some of Kate's natural good humor returned as she considered how hard Lois had pushed for that approval. "You didn't leave him much choice. At one point I thought you were going to beat him over the head with that layout."

"He deserved it. Imagine acting like that at his age."

"Eight or eighty, men always seem to act the same."

Lois's eyes narrowed slightly. "It isn't like you to be cynical."

No, it wasn't. But Kate had to admit, if only silently, that she was often not like herself lately. Pregnancy was turning out to be much more complicated than she had expected. She was finding herself in the midst of a completely unanticipated upheaval.

As if the transformation of her body weren't enough, her mind seemed to be affected as well. She felt much more emotional and vulnerable than she had at any time since adolescence. Several times in the last few weeks she had suddenly begun crying for no apparent reason.

Once Adam had found her huddled in a chair, sobbing helplessly. As soon as he was able to determine that there was nothing actually wrong with her, he had held and soothed her gently until she quieted. Not for a moment did he show the slightest impatience with her moods. In fact, he was so tolerant and understanding that Kate almost longed for a flash of healthy temper. He made her feel as though she had no more substance than the thinnest piece of glass and could shatter into a thousand fragments without warning.

That wasn't at all how she thought of herself. She was a strong, capable woman, used to being very much in control of both her body and mind. But suddenly she was neither.

At lunchtime Kate decided she needed a break. She had barely been outside the building in days. The rushing, pushing crowds that thronged the narrow sidewalks at noon still put her off, but she was determined to persevere. Slipping into the jacket of the mauve linen suit she had worn that day, she told Pete she would be back soon and headed for the elevator.

First on the agenda was a hot dog smothered in onions from one of the fast-food carts parked at almost every corner. The first hot dog was so good that she quickly ate another, to the amusement of the grizzled vendor.

"You like those so much," he said, "how come I haven't seen you here before?"

Kate didn't have the heart to tell him she wouldn't normally be caught dead eating what she had just devoured with such delight. Instead she murmured something about being new in town, resisted the urge to purchase a soft pretzel for dessert, and left.

New York was experiencing one of its rare perfect spring days. Not a cloud marred the cobalt sky, which was reflected in the wide sweep of glass and steel towers along Fifth Avenue. The air, sweetly perfumed by the scents of new grass and flowers drifting down from nearby Central Park, seemed washed clean by the recent rain.

Even the hordes of office workers pouring out of every door had thrown off their winter grayness. The pace of the human current ebbing and flowing along the streets was slower than usual. Men walked with their suit jackets pushed back or draped over their arms. They lounged in front of buildings, watching pretty young women wearing bright spring outfits and high heels that showed off their legs.

Remembering that her own wardrobe could use some refurbishing, Kate ventured into one of the elegant department stores lining the avenue. She drifted desultorily among the racks until she spied a suit in chocolate brown linen with an amber silk blouse. The outfit was not only perfect for her coloring but also affordable.

In the dressing room she quickly shed her outer clothes and slipped into the blouse and skirt, only to check the ticket hastily. Though they were both her usual size ten, neither fit. The silk gapped at her breasts, and the waistband was so tight as to be unbearable.

Dismay flashed through her, only to vanish instantly as she laughed at her own foolishness. Of couse they wouldn't fit. Willy was taking up more and more

# Gilded Spring 89

room every day. Already her breasts were not only more sensitive but also larger. Her narrow waist had begun to fill out, and there was a small bulge where her flat abdomen had once been. She would just have to make do with the more generously cut clothes she already owned until she could start shopping for maternity dresses.

Hanging the suit back up without a flicker of regret, she detoured through the toy department before returning reluctantly to the office. She had barely sat down when Pete popped his head around the door to announce, "Adam called. I told him you were out for a walk."

"Okay. Any other messages?"

"Yes, they're on your desk." He hesitated, watching her flip through the slips of paper. She decided they could wait until later in the day. When she made no move to reach for the phone, Pete asked, "Aren't you going to call him back?"

"Him who?"

"Adam, of course."

"Sure I will, but does it have to be right this minute?"

"I think that would be a good idea. When he heard you were out by yourself, he was worried."

Kate stifled a groan. She was in too good a mood to get annoyed at Pete, but Adam was another story. "If I call him now, will you stop pestering me?"

"Yes."

"Then it's a deal."

She waited until Pete discreetly withdrew before placing the call. The pointed comment she had intended to make about her husband's overprotectiveness faded the moment she heard his voice. He sounded so relieved that she couldn't bring herself to distress him.

Instead she said, "Hi. You're talking to a lady who had two hot dogs for lunch and then was surprised to discover she couldn't fit into a size ten skirt anymore."

Adam's ready laughter told her he had been as concerned about how she would react to his checking up on her as about her absence. "Should I assume that you're feeling better?" he asked.

"Well, let me put it this way. What would you say to having chili for dinner tonight?"

"I'd say you're out of your gorgeous mind. Do you really think it's a good idea to push your luck?"

"No, I suppose not. I'll settle for pepperoni grinders."

His heartfelt moan made her giggle. But her laughter faded when he added, "You need a keeper."

She didn't doubt he thought so, but she also didn't want to pursue that topic over the phone. Instead she assured him once again that she was fine, she would be waiting downstairs when he arrived, and if she felt tired during the afternoon, she would rest.

As it turned out, she had a burst of energy that carried her through to five o'clock and enabled her to accomplish far more than she had hoped. By the time she said good night to Pete, she had made real progress at refining the Femme campaign.

The deadline for the presentation to the client was fast approaching, but she was no longer as concerned about meeting it. Experience had long ago taught her that most projects lurched and staggered along to completion, while a chosen few progressed smoothly right

# Gilded Spring 91

from the start. Although she was hardly naive enough to think there would be no problems with Femme, the campaign was showing signs of encountering far fewer difficulties than usual.

She was smiling at that thought when Adam deftly maneuvered their fire-engine-red Volkswagen between a double-parked truck and a bus to pull up at the curb right in front of her. Through the windshield she saw him impatiently push aside a lock of chestnut hair that had fallen across his forehead. The sun had added a ruddy glow to his chiseled cheeks. The slight shadow of several hours' growth of beard emphasized the sensual line of his mouth.

He had tossed his suit jacket in the back, and his broad shoulders and powerful chest were clearly revealed by his crisp white shirt. He looked deliciously male and eminently desirable, or so Kate thought as she slid into the car and brushed a light kiss across his lean cheek.

"How's the best pickup service in New York this evening?"

"Watch it, lady. If my wife catches you doing that, she'll cream you."

"*Wife?* You never told me you were married."

Wiggling his eyebrows, he sighed. "Did I forget to mention that? Gee, I'm sorry. Can't imagine how it slipped my mind."

Eluding the gearshift, she moved close enough to trace her long fingernails down the back of his neck between the neatly trimmed line of his hair and the starched collar of his shirt. "Maybe I'll have to come up with some way of helping you remember," she suggested provocatively.

Adam leered encouragingly, ignoring the irate blare of a horn as he cut in front of a taxi. "Got any ideas?"

"Mmm, lots..." She teased his earlobe with cool lips, then nipped at it with her teeth.

"Stop that!" he demanded as he struggled to keep his hands on the wheel.

"Why? We're going to be here as long as that light is red."

"Yeah, but not long enough for what you're making me want, so cut it out."

Reluctantly Kate obeyed, but only briefly. When they stopped again several blocks later, she couldn't resist the urge to resume her enticing assault. Slipping her hand down the front of his shirt, she swiftly undid enough buttons to give her access to the smooth expanse of his chest. Dropping teasing kisses along his jaw, she deliberately allowed her finger to brush against the flat male nipples that hardened at her touch.

*"Kate!"*

"Mmm?"

The light changed. She withdrew her hand as Adam growled in frustration. "Wait until I get you home," he threatened, his attempt to sound menacing somewhat spoiled by the anticipatory gleam in his eyes.

"Promises, promises."

"More than that, sweetheart." Speeding up slightly, he managed to make the next series of lights, giving her no further opportunity to continue her seduction.

Kate didn't mind. She was satisfied with the results so far and content to wait for more. At least so long as they didn't get caught in any traffic jams. Since she could no longer count on how her body would

## Gilded Spring 93

feel from one day to the next, she intended to make the most of her present mood.

Clearly Adam had the same thought. He made the trip in the shortest possible time, swinging into the garage down the block from their house a good ten minutes earlier than usual. Even so, Kate was out of the car and heading up the stairs to the house before he could collect his briefcase and jacket from the backseat.

"Hey, wait up," he called after her.

Sending him a provocative grin over her shoulder, she kept going. Adam's eyes narrowed determinedly. As he followed her up to the bedroom, he began methodically shedding his clothes. By the time he pushed open the door, his tie was gone and he was pulling his unbuttoned shirt out of his pants.

But Kate had gone him one better. She sat in the middle of the bed, wearing only a gossamer lace and silk robe that made her nudity underneath all the more provocative. Her glistening blond hair tumbled around her shoulders. Desire mingled with a lingering bashfulness gave her face a radiant glow.

Adam stopped short at the door, drinking in the sight of her. A blatantly male grin of anticipation lit his eyes as he walked slowly toward her, unfastening his belt.

"Planning to nap before dinner?" he asked.

"Not exactly."

"Want your back rubbed?"

"Among other things."

His pants joined his shirt on the floor, and he slid into bed beside her. His large hand ran lightly down the sleeve of her robe as he fingered the material. "Not much to this, is there?"

Kate shifted slightly so that the sheer silk fell open to reveal the bare expanse of her slender legs. She raised her arm, letting the lace-cuffed sleeve drift across his chest.

"It's more than you're wearing."

Reaching for her, he murmured thickly, "I was about to point that out."

The robe soon joined his clothes on the floor as their bodies entwined. Adam pressed her carefully into the mattress. Propped up on his elbows, holding fistfuls of her hair, he dropped feather-light kisses at the corners of her eyes, along the bridge of her nose, and around the curve of her chin—everywhere except on the parted lips that yearned for him.

Only when Kate was breathing hard, her hands digging into the sculpted muscles of his back, did he at last bring their mouths together. A whimper of spiraling desire broke from her as his tongue plunged deeply, tasting the moist sweetness she offered.

Against the hair-roughened hardness of his chest, her nipples grew dark and taut. When he at last drew back to survey the effect of his caresses, they beckoned his touch unashamedly.

A husky laugh sounded far down in his throat. "So beautiful—and mine."

Kate gloried in his possessiveness, beyond any glimmer of resentment for the purely male instinct that drove him to claim her fully. She arched closer to him, warm and pliant, as he traced the delicate line of her ribs with his mouth before lapping gently at her navel.

## Gilded Spring

"Adam—please—"

Though he was almost mindless with passion, he refused to heed her entreaty. Instead he grasped her waist and, moving so swiftly that she could not resist, turned her over.

Holding her gently but firmly beneath him, he used his powerful legs and arms to keep her in place while his mouth traced the ultrasensitive line of her spine. Wave after wave of intense pleasure swept over Kate as he let his teeth rack over the hollows between her shoulder blades.

Perfectly gauging her endurance, he knew exactly when to tenderly thrust his knee between her legs and open her for him. Lifting her slightly from the bed, he entered her with great care, not moving within her until he was absolutely certain she was ready.

Together they drew out their ascent to the utmost until desire strummed liked a finely drawn chord within them and the world exploded into shimmering fragments of ecstasy.

## 8

"I'VE DECIDED YOU'RE not the only one in the family with musical talent," Kate announced the next morning as she and Adam were getting dressed for work.

"Oh, lord! You don't mean you're going to start singing in the morning, too, do you?"

"Yep. Morning—afternoon—evening—middle of the night. Those are all good times for a little harmonizing."

"Only one problem, pet." He laughed. "We both know that you can't—"

"Carry a tune with a wheelbarrow," Kate interrupted good-naturedly. "Too true. But then the kindest description of your musical renditions that comes to mind is tone deaf. Poor Willy. I'm afraid a great operatic career isn't in the cards for our offspring."

"Oh, I don't know. Heredity is a funny thing. Willy might turn out to be a regular songbird."

"If he does," Kate murmured, "I won't blame you for looking at me a bit skeptically."

Adam grinned. He ruffled her hair gently. "No, I wouldn't. I think you're capable of accomplishing absolutely anything, even a singing Willy."

Kate glanced at him quickly. He meant it. His faith

warmed her all the way through. She was still smiling as they climbed into the car for the drive to Manhattan.

"Have you given any thought to what you'd like for your birthday?" Adam asked as he maneuvered through traffic.

"No," Kate admitted. She hesitated before suggesting, "Why don't we just skip it this year?"

"You're not serious."

He looked so surprised that she couldn't help but laugh. At thirty-five Adam still celebrated his birthdays with all the enthusiasm of an eight-year-old, perhaps because when he was a child the occasion had more often than not passed unnoticed. Understanding that, Kate went to great lengths to find exactly the right presents and invite friends over for parties.

But when it came to her own birthday, she took a different view. While she fully agreed that women only got better as they got older, she still preferred to slip into her thirties with a minimum of fuss.

"It's really not a big deal to me," she explained. "I'd just as soon forget about it."

Adam regarded her skeptically. "You're not self-conscious about turning thirty, are you?"

"No, of course not," she denied quickly. "Well—maybe a little."

Adam chuckled softly. "Believe me, honey, on you thirty looks great." His grin widened as he added, "I'll bet eighty or ninety will, too."

Though she pretended to disregard his flattery, she was secretly pleased by it. After five years of marriage and with a baby on the way, it was reassuring to know her husband still found her desirable. However, she wasn't swayed enough to reveal any wish for a birthday celebration.

Not one to be easily discouraged, Adam informed her that he would simply have to come up with a present on his own. As he dropped her off at the office, he gave her a last chance to change her mind. "You know, if you let me handle this, I'm liable to decide on something really tasteless."

"Totally unredeemable?" Kate asked, getting out of the car.

"Absolutely."

"Good, I'll leave you to it." Laughing at his look of chagrin, she kissed him lightly. Minutes later she was riding up in the elevator, having put all thought of her impending birthday firmly out of her mind.

By Friday Kate had genuinely forgotten their discussion. Adam, however, had not. He could barely contain his excitement when he picked her up that afternoon. As he began driving through the rush of commuters heading home for the weekend, he said casually, "So how's everything at the office?"

The very blandness of his tone was enough to catch her attention. Eyeing him more closely, she said, "All right. How about you?"

"Fine, fine. No problems."

"That's good. Anything special going on?"

"No! I mean, what makes you ask that?"

Kate chuckled softly. As the usual end-of-the-week fog lifted from her mind, she remembered that her birthday was the next day. Adam must have gone ahead and planned something, a surprise party perhaps, or maybe dinner at a really extravagant restaurant.

Deciding that neither of those would be too hard to take, she said, "Oh, nothing, except that you look like you're about to jump out of your skin with excitement." Fondly she added, "It's a good thing you don't play poker. You'd never be able to bluff."

Grinning ruefully, he admitted she was right. "But you don't know what I've planned."

"I'll bet I can guess."

"Bet you can't."

"That's what I like about our marriage—we have such mature discussions."

"Don't try to change the subject," Adam warned, "unless you want to give up before you even start."

"No way! Let's see—we're going to Windows on the World for dinner."

"Nope."

"You invited some friends over and they're all hiding in our living room."

"Wrong again."

"Ummm." Kate thought for a moment before her face lit up. "I know. You bought me some lingerie from one of those really sexy catalogs."

"Now that's a great idea. Too bad I didn't think of it."

Running out of guesses, she asked, "What did you think of?"

Speeding up to avoid a red light, he shook his head and shot her a teasing grin. "I'm not going to tell you."

"*Adam!* That's not fair."

## Gilded Spring 101

"Sure it is. Anyway, you'll have much more fun figuring it out."

Flopping back in her seat, Kate gave an exaggerated sigh. She made several more attempts to find out what he was planning, but Adam wouldn't budge. Finally lapsing into silence, she gazed out the window sightlessly until it slowly dawned on her that they weren't taking the usual route home.

Straightening, she asked, "Is there something wrong with the traffic?"

He grinned at her provocatively. "Not so far as I can see."

Kate made a face at him. "Then why are we on this road?"

"Because it happens to go where we're going."

"Which is—?"

With mock exasperation Adam said, "Don't you know kidnap victims are supposed to be quiet and not ask a lot of questions?"

Kate's mouth dropped open. She had been prepared for a lot of possibilities, but not this. "Is that what you're doing—kidnapping me?"

"Yes. Now hush up and let me concentrate. I've never abducted anyone before and I want to get it right."

He seemed to be making a pretty good job of it, she thought a few minutes later as he maneuvered the car down an entrance ramp to the Long Island Expressway and set it heading firmly east. Kate's puzzlement continued to deepen as mile after mile sped by.

Only when they had passed through the densely packed suburbs clustered on the edge of the city and reached the more open, rural stretches that would continue as far as the island's tip did she begin to suspect where they might be going.

Slowly she asked, "Did you bring along luggage by any chance?"

"I was wondering when you'd ask about that." Adam chortled. "If you look in the backseat under my jacket, you'll find both our bags. I packed enough for a weekend."

"Then we must be going to the inn."

"That's right. What self-respecting kidnapper would take you anywhere else?"

Unable to contain her exuberance, Kate threw her arms around him and kissed him soundly. They had honeymooned at the Breakers Inn overlooking Montauk Point and had returned there several times since then. Each visit stood out in her mind as a special interlude of love and tenderness. She was deeply touched that Adam had thought of it.

When they at last pulled up in front of the rambling clapboard house set on a bluff overlooking the ocean, she scrambled eagerly out of the car. Adam insisted on carrying all the baggage, but it was light enough for him to manage with one hand while she held the other. Together they strolled up the flower-lined path to the door.

The entry hall was very quiet. Kate took a deep breath, savoring the fragrances of salt air, pine trees, and lemon polish. Nothing had changed since their last visit. There was still the same choice collection of antiques furnishing the vestibule, the same muted oriental rugs covering the wide plank floor, even the

# Gilded Spring

same air of elegant graciousness for which the inn was justly renowned.

At the registration desk they were welcomed by the son of the owners, who remembered them from previous visits. When he said how nice it was to see them back, both Kate and Adam could honestly reply that the pleasure was theirs.

The gentle lapping of waves against the nearby beach, the haunting cry of sea gulls circling overhead, and the distant sound of a Mozart concerto playing softly in the kitchen were far removed from the blare of city traffic and the loud voices of New York inhabitants.

The hectic pace of the city seemed light-years away from the slow swaying of scrub grass in the gentle breeze, the ruffling of white curtains at the window of their room, and the leisurely sense of time itself slowing down.

When they had unpacked and changed into more comfortable clothes, they took a walk along the beach, pausing often to admire the sculpted curve of sand dunes, the opalescent perfection of shells caught in clumps of glistening seaweed, the delicate froth of sea foam catching at their feet, and the wisps of clouds drifting across the turquoise sky.

A deep sense of contentment spread through Kate. Tension she had hardly been aware of slipped away, leaving her more at peace than she remembered being in a long time.

Her head rested on Adam's shoulder as they walked with his arm wrapped around her waist. The rough wool of his jacket brushed against her cheek. She could feel the leashed power of his muscles even through her clothes. The intrinsically male scent of soap, aftershave, and burnished skin teased her nostrils. When she closed her eyes briefly, she was engulfed by an almost overpowering sensation of virile strength and gentleness.

She raised thick lashes to meet his gaze. They spoke as one. "Let's go back to the room."

Slipping quietly up the stairs, they closed the door firmly behind them before turning into each other's arms. Sweaters, jeans, jackets, underwear all fell onto the floor in a heap. Laughing, they tumbled across the bed, vying to find the most susceptible pleasure points and inflict the greatest delight.

Sunlight filtering through the sheer white curtains drifted across limbs entwined in loving torment. Kate turned her head into the pillows to stifle her cries as Adam tenderly caressed her sensitive breasts with his hands and lips. When his hot, moist mouth tugged gently on a nipple, she arched helplessly against him.

Trailing burning kisses down the slight bulge of her abdomen, he savored the silken skin of her inner thighs before his fingers tangled gently in the cluster of curls sheltering her womanhood. Carefully but relentlessly he drove her to the furthest limits of rapture before at last giving in to his own surging need and releasing himself deep within her.

Even then they did not move apart but remained cradled in each other's arms, sleeping until dinner time.

Waking in the quiet of the evening, Kate was momentarily uncertain where she was. Adam's quiet breathing beside her quickly banished her confusion

## Gilded Spring

and brought a blush of memory to her cheeks. Smiling gently, she traced a finger over his lips, which were relaxed in sleep.

All the deep, abiding love she felt for him welled up in her, almost frightening in its intensity. More than ever before, she was forced to acknowledge the full extent of her dependency on him. Commonplace wisdom proclaimed it wrong for any woman to make a man the focus of her life. Yet she couldn't help herself. He was as much a part of her as the child growing in her womb.

She couldn't honestly say she would want it any other way. Far from detracting from her individuality, she knew that Adam's faith in her was a big factor in helping her achieve her full potential, even as she tried her best to help him do the same. In their marriage the whole truly was more than the parts. And now there was a child coming to make the total even greater.

Sighing happily, Kate brushed a gentle kiss across Adam's mouth and watched his eyes flick open. His warm gaze revealed instant recollection of the joy they had shared such a short time before.

Huskily he murmured, "Hello, there. Are you by any chance the same faintly harassed-looking lady I scooped off a sidewalk in New York this afternoon?"

"Nope," Kate teased. "She left. I am a lady of leisure with nothing to do but please herself and"—she trailed a hand down his broad chest, letting her fingers twine in the thick mat of hair that tapered across his flat abdomen—"her husband."

"Lucky me." Adam growled, reaching for her.

Laughing, she eluded his grasp and slipped from

the bed. "But first you have to feed me. I'm starved."

"Glutton."

"Hear that, Willy? Your father thinks we're chow-hounds."

"I think you're a stark-naked siren who should come back here."

"Later, after I've been fed. Otherwise I might be tempted to chew on you."

Adam laughed but gave in to her. A short time later they were seated at a candlelit table overlooking the ocean, enjoying superb clam chowder, fresh baked rolls, grilled trout, endive salad, and a sinfully rich apple pie topped with homemade vanilla ice cream.

Throughout dinner they talked easily about nothing in particular. By tacit agreement neither of them mentioned work or anything else remotely serious. Only when they were finishing dessert did Adam surprise Kate by saying, "I've been giving some thought to remodeling the guest room. It's big enough for a nursery, don't you think, and close enough to us so that we'll hear the baby when he cries at night."

Since Kate herself had not yet gotten around to thinking of such things, she was surprised he had. Adam had never shown any inclination to tackle projects around the house. Whenever something needed doing, he called in a professional, claiming it was cheaper in the end. Now all of a sudden he was talking about decorating the nursery himself.

Not sure that she was hearing right, Kate said, "Let me get this straight. *You're* going to do all the painting, wallpapering, and so on?"

Adam nodded, as though that were the most natural

thing in the world. "Of course. I also thought some built-in shelves and maybe a changing table would help."

Misinterpreting her astounded look, he added hastily, "Oh, don't worry. I'm not proposing to leave you out entirely. You can pick the curtains and other things like that."

Kate shook her head in amazement. "This I have to see. As far as I know, you aren't sure which end of a hammer does what."

Adam tried to look offended but only managed to grin. "I'll learn. Besides, Ray offered to help. Between the two of us, we'll do fine."

Visions of chaos darted through Kate's mind. Carol held the rare distinction of having cajoled both an electrician and a plumber into working on a Sunday by explaining that her nuclear-engineer husband had almost blown up their home while trying to install a self-heating baby bath. She still claimed that their son had arrived a week early because of that incident.

"Is that the same Ray who almost single-handedly wrecked their entire apartment while working in Davey's nursery?"

"Never mind," Adam said firmly. "You just concentrate on the baby and I'll take care of the rest."

As they went on to speak of other topics, Kate couldn't suppress an occasional grin. The image of Adam struggling with ceiling mobiles, fairy-tale decals, and other nursery paraphernalia was too good to relinquish. Especially since she already suspected she wouldn't be able to talk him out of it.

Declining the offer of afterdinner drinks, they

wrapped up warmly to take another stroll along the beach before falling into bed happily tired and utterly at peace with themselves and each other.

Neither cared that it rained the next day. Kate woke with a touch of the nausea she had been experiencing off and on, but it disappeared in time for her to join Adam at breakfast. They returned to their room to find the fireplace laid with fresh kindling. Taking that as a hint as to how to spend the soggy morning, they quickly had a cheerful blaze going.

Curled up in front of it, Kate read a romantic novel she had picked up downstairs while Adam continued to study his baby book. From time to time he interrupted to share information he considered particularly important.

"Did you know that during the last months of pregnancy, a baby can hear sounds in the womb and may even be able to see light through his mother's skin?"

"Oh... that's nice..."

"Don't you think that's incredible?"

"What? Oh, yes, of course, it's fantastic."

"Not only that, but do you know that right after he's born he'll automatically try to walk if held upright? He loses that after a while and doesn't regain it for months, but it's fascinating to think the instinct is present at the beginning."

"Great. The sooner he walks, the sooner he can get a job."

*"Kate,* aren't you interested in this at all?"

Looking up from her book, she realized that Adam was perturbed by her failure to share his enthusiasm. Teasingly she said, "I'm sorry, Adam, but the heroine of this story is about to be ravished by a fierce pirate captain who is really a disguised English lord, and I have to find out what will happen. Anyway, why do you keep calling the baby he? Willy might be a girl."

That thought silenced him momentarily. Slowly he asked, "A girl? Do you really think so?"

Swallowing a giggle, Kate said patiently, "There's a fifty-fifty chance."

"Maybe not. There haven't been any girls born in my family for a couple of generations."

"Then you're overdue. Besides, wouldn't you like a daughter?"

"Of course I would. I just hadn't thought..."

Watching him, Kate could almost see the abrupt reassessment going on in his mind. He was trying to switch from pictures of himself teaching a son to play baseball and climb trees to images of a little girl in frilly dresses and curls.

"Don't worry," she said quickly. "It won't be all that different if we have a daughter. Nowadays boys and girls do more of the same things than we did when we were little."

"I suppose so, but what about later?"

"Later?"

"When she gets older—and guys start hanging around. They'll probably try to keep her out to all hours, get her into the backseat of cars, convince her to—" Running a hand through his hair, he scowled ominously. "By God, I'll take a horsewhip to the first one who tries it! She's not dating until she's eighteen, and she's not staying out late no matter how old she is. Got that?"

Holding tight to the laughter that threatened to erupt at any moment, Kate managed to nod somberly. "Got it. Remind me to check our supply of horsewhips, and while I'm at it, maybe I should get you a shotgun, just in case."

"It's not funny!"

"Oh, Adam, of course it is! The baby hasn't even been born yet and already you're worried about her virtue." Wryly she added, "How come you were never so concerned about mine?"

Giving in to her gentle kidding, he relaxed enough to respond in kind. "Oh, but I was concerned—that you were going to insist on holding onto it."

"Fat chance! I seem to remember you sweeping me off my feet and into bed before I knew what hit me."

"Any regrets?"

"No," she admitted softly. "Never."

His eyes were very tender as he nodded. "Me neither."

Snuggled close together by the fire, they spent the rest of the morning quietly reading before venturing out for a short walk in the rain after lunch. Back in their room, Kate was beginning to feel at loose ends when Adam pulled a pack of cards out of his bag.

"How about a game of Uno?" he suggested.

"Okay."

"Good. I've got a special version in mind."

The gleam in his eye warned Kate. "Oh?"

"You've heard of strip poker?"

"Not only heard, I've also played it many times."

"Liar. But if you're feeling so bold, then you

# Gilded Spring    111

shouldn't object to taking your clothes off for me."

"What makes you think I'll lose?" Kate demanded as she hastily cleared a spot in front of the fire.

"Because I'm planning to cheat."

"Hah! I'll still win."

Shuffling the cards, Adam leered at her challengingly. "We'll see."

Two hands later Kate had been forced to shed her shoes, but so had Adam. Moments later he lost his socks as she chortled. "Told you so."

"It's early yet."

A few minutes later she not only had to peel off her socks but also remove the belt from her jeans.

"Now we're getting somewhere," he said with a satisfied growl.

"Says you." Slapping down a winning hand, she watched with equal satisfaction as he disgruntledly peeled off his sweater. Silently vowing that the shirt he wore under it would go next, she was disappointed when the cards turned against her and she was forced to shed her blouse.

"No fair," she protested, moving closer to the fire to keep warm. "You've got more clothes on."

"You're welcome to check, but I promise I'm not wearing a bra."

Moments later he was proven correct as his shirt joined hers on the floor.

"This is starting to get interesting," Adam said, dealing another hand. His eyes were on the golden glow of her skin as he quickly won again. Leaning back, he demanded, "Those jeans have to go."

"You're a hard man," she protested, removing the slacks.

Gazing at the slender form covered only by her scant bra and panties, he nodded. "I'm getting there."

Kate flushed slightly, then laughed when the next hand went to her. "Speaking of jeans..."

He removed them swiftly, apparently eager to get on with it. His dedication was rewarded when he won the next round. "Now then..."

His look was so heated that she shifted under it. Unaccountably self-conscious, she hesitated before reluctantly unhooking her bra and removing it. A dark flush stained her cheeks as, despite the warmth of the fire, her nipples hardened.

He was so pleasantly preoccupied with watching her that she had to remind him to deal the cards. Before the next hand could be played, Adam moved closer. His fingers lightly stroked the ripe curve of one breast before fastening gently on the taut peak.

Kate shivered, but not with cold. She made a valiant effort to keep her attention on the game, only to fail utterly when his mouth replaced his hand as he tenderly suckled her.

"D-don't you want to play anymore?"

"Sure do." Taking her cards, he tossed them along with his on the floor and carefully eased her back. What followed was a revelation in her own capacity for passion. Whether it was because she was unusually relaxed or because Adam was determined to bring her to the point of greatest possible pleasure, or a combination of both, Kate found herself engulfed in wave after wave of undulating sensations that ignited a firestorm deep within her.

He held her gently as he stroked and caressed every inch of her body. Beginning with the delicate hollows

## Gilded Spring          113

behind her ears and at the base of her throat, he went on to savor the fullness of each ripe breast, the indentation of her waist, the slightly swollen curve of her belly, and the taut line of her thighs. When his mouth reached her calves, he grasped her ankles firmly and spread them apart.

A piercing sense of vulnerability shot through her, making her try to draw her legs together, but Adam would not allow it. His tongue savored the ultrasensitive back of her knees before moving up to the silken skin of her inner thighs. Inexorbably he claimed the secret place that sheltered their child, bringing her to a peak of pleasure so intense that Kate had to bite down on her hand to keep a scream of ecstasy from escaping.

When she had recovered enough to understand that he had not yet entered her, she urged him to do so. But instead, he resumed his loving assault on her body, bringing her to fulfillment again and again before at last giving in to her plea for the ultimate union. Long after he had groaned her name into her mouth at the moment of his own completion, aftershocks continued to quake through her. She was barely aware when Adam lifted her onto the bed and covered them both.

As they had the previous day, they slept until dinnertime, then rose and dressed slowly. Hand in hand they strolled down to the dining room to share another exquisite meal. At its completion a beaming waiter presented Kate with a chocolate birthday cake, and all the guests joined in singing "Happy Birthday" in a genially raucous medley that threatened to shake the aged walls.

Kate was still laughing when they made their way back upstairs. She was about to tell Adam that it was the best birthday she had ever had when he made it even better by presenting her with a small, flat box wrapped in silver paper. Opening it, she found a beautiful topaz pendant that perfectly complemented the golden glints of her deep brown eyes.

The pendant rested between her naked breasts when, much later, they at last drifted to sleep nestled in each other's arms.

Far into the night, Kate woke suddenly. Some disturbing thought had driven her back to consciousness. She lay staring up at the canopy until she was slowly able to identify the cause of her unease.

The hours she had just spent with Adam were infinitely precious to her. She wouldn't have missed them for the world. But along with all the joy they brought also came a disquieting concern.

Would such closeness still be possible as her pregnancy became more and more obvious? Or would they become so caught up in their impending roles as parents that they would forget that they were first and foremost husband and wife?

The moment the thought surfaced, Kate was ashamed. Was she really so insecure that she could fear the influence of her own child? Was her relationship with Adam so shallow as to be threatened by the inevitable changes the baby would bring?

Determinedly she told herself that wasn't the case. Their love for each other had proved itself over and over through five years. There was no reason to think

# Gilded Spring

it would be anything other than enlarged and strengthened by their child.

Still, although she believed all that, misgivings continued to haunt her.

# 9

"YOUR WEEKEND SEEMS to have done you some good," Lois said when she dropped by Kate's office early Monday morning. "You certainly look better."

Hoping no one would notice the blush that spread quickly over her cheeks, Kate said noncommittally, "It was okay. How about yours?"

Lois grimaced. "I spent it going over another of the agency's troublesome accounts. You remember the one for doggie breath cleaner?"

"I sure do. I hid out in the supply room for a week while you were deciding which writer would work on it."

"Smart girl. Anyway, we ended up hiring a freelancer because no one on staff would touch it. The poor guy did his best, but what can you say about canine mouthwash?"

"Takes the stink out of the woof?"

"Hmmm...that's no worse than what we've already got. Maybe I should have given this to you after all."

Groaning, Kate muttered, "I think I feel a migraine coming on."

"That's an occupational hazard, along with ulcers; but how are you feeling otherwise?"

"Pretty good. I had another bout of the queasies this morning, and I don't think I'm in any mood to run a marathon, but other than that, everything's fine."

"I'm glad to hear it." Lois grinned as she added, "I think you should know there's already an office pool taking bets on when Willy will arrive."

Kate's eyes widened. She had known her colleagues were interested in her condition, but she hadn't realized they were going quite that far. "Let me guess. Did Pete start it?"

"Uh-huh. I understand he's already collected quite a pot."

Glancing down at the bulge beneath her skirt, Kate sighed. "He's not the only one."

Lois laughed. "Beginning to spread?"

"I'll say. According to the pamphlets the doctor gave me, this isn't supposed to happen for a couple of months yet." Her gaze darkened as she muttered, "I wouldn't put it past Adam to have gotten me with twins."

"I'm sure the dear man is quite capable of it, but you really shouldn't worry. Everybody reacts differently at the beginning. My sister always feels more comfortable in maternity clothes by her third month."

"I may go shopping for some soon. To tell the truth, I'm kind of looking forward to it."

"Of course you are. Something very special is happening to you. Why be shy about it?"

"Oh, I don't know exactly. It's just that this is so different from anything I've ever been through. Everything else that's good in my life came about so differently that this has me stunned."

## Gilded Spring 119

Lois frowned slightly, trying to follow her. "What do you mean?"

"Well, with my career and even my marriage—I've worked at those, made decisions, planned, all that sort of thing. But with the baby, once it started, it just kept going of its own accord without my having to do anything."

"And that throws you?"

"It sure does. I may be the one doing the carrying, but I feel like I'm just along for the ride."

"I think I see what you mean," Lois said slowly. "We're both used to having a fair amount of control over our lives. If I felt that control slipping away, I guess it would bother me too."

"It's not just the lack of control I mind. There's also the fact that I'm engaged in an enormously complicated task of creating a child cell by cell and organ by organ, yet I have nothing conscious to do with it. A whole side of me I've never had any reason to notice before is busily working away on some level I can't begin to understand."

Lois laughed softly. Her eyes were warm as she studied Kate. "It's called instincts, honey. Be glad we've got them."

"Oh, I am. But it's a little scary, too. It's enough to have the baby growing inside me. When I add this entirely unknown part of myself, I start to feel more than a little crowded."

"What an image." Lois laughed. "You make it sound like a circus in there."

"Believe me, that's how it feels sometimes. A three-ring circus with my stomach bouncing around on a trampoline and my head flying back and forth on the trapeze. Now all I need are a few clowns."

"Then you're in the right business. We're top-heavy with them."

Wondering if Lois was having one of her down-on-advertising days, Kate asked, "Do you have anyone in particular in mind?"

"A certain silver-haired gentleman. But I can't really blame him for my mood. It's just my annual case of spring fever." Grinning, she added, "At least we know that isn't what's wrong with you."

"Well, it is, sort of," Kate claimed guilelessly. "After all, I am budding."

Lois groaned and on that note departed. Kate spent the next several hours fine-tuning parts of the Femme campaign, which was due to be presented to the client at the end of the week. She wanted to make it as close to perfect as possible before then. But the memory of the weekend she had spent with Adam, and the troubling thoughts that occupied her mind, continued to distract her. The closer she got to quitting time, the more eager she was to see Adam, if only to reassure herself that what they had shared over the last few days was real.

But just as she was packing up to leave, he called to say he had to work late. "I'm sorry, honey, but a big problem just cropped up and it's got to be handled immediately."

"Oh... well, that's all right. I understand. I'll take the bus home."

"Why don't you take a cab instead?"

"That's awfully extravagant." Why was she objecting to something so inconsequential when she was really upset about having to spend the evening alone? Sighing, Kate added, "But never mind, I'll get a taxi. Will you want dinner when you get home?"

"I don't think so. We'll probably just send out for sandwiches or something."

Great, that meant he really expected to be late. But how could she complain about it when she knew Adam never neglected their time together unless he had absolutely no choice? Besides, it wasn't as though the shoe hadn't been on the other foot often enough.

"Okay, I'll expect you when I see you."

Though she tried to keep the regret out of her voice, she didn't quite succeed. Adam caught a hint of it and said quickly, "If I'm going to be later than nine or so, I'll call you again."

"I'd appreciate that," Kate replied. She hung up, telling herself she should be more grateful for his thoughtfulness. After all, plenty of women couldn't be sure where their husbands were when they claimed to be working late. She had enough friends who had cried on her shoulder because their marriages were threatened by infidelity to know how lucky she was to have escaped that problem.

But even knowing that Adam was in all ways a terrific friend, lover, and husband, she couldn't entirely stifle her resentment at having to share him with his work just when she needed him most. It was selfish of her, she knew, and she had no intention of revealing her feelings to him. Yet that night she caught herself watching the clock when she was trying to pay attention to the television set, and grew increasingly impatient as the hours ticked by with no sign of Adam.

When the phone rang shortly after nine o'clock,

she reached for it reluctantly.

"I'm afraid it's shaping up to be an all-nighter," Adam said. "One of the main computers blew, and if we don't recover the lost data by morning, we'll be in a hell of a fix when the market opens."

"I understand," Kate assured him automatically. She knew he wouldn't exaggerate the importance of the problem any more than he would stay at work out of some overblown sense of loyalty to the company. He was probably thinking about the clients who depended on him for both insightful guidance and prompt action. It wasn't in him to let them down if there was any alternative.

They talked for only a few moments more before he returned to work and she settled back down in front of the TV, staring at it sightlessly. A sigh of impatience escaped her as she abruptly snapped it off and went upstairs. Curled up in bed, she tried to read, but she was feeling unaccountably nervous and couldn't concentrate on the novel she had chosen.

Every sound the old house made seemed amplified tenfold in the stillness. Every creak of a wall or floorboard, every sound drifting up the stairwell, every unexplained noise brought her sitting upright. Since she was a little girl, Kate had never minded being by herself, and she was at a loss to understand her sudden nervousness now. One of Dr. Thorpe's pamphlets warned that pregnant women were likely to experience anxiety attacks, but she hadn't thought such a thing could happen to *her*.

After padding downstairs she heated a cup of milk and drank it slowly. Glancing out the window, she could see that the streets were deserted. In a neighborhood where most people rose early for work, only a scattering of house lights still shone.

She sat at the butcher-block table and considered how few of the people who lived in the nearby houses she actually knew. Back home in Long Island, she had grown up surrounded by an extended family of relatives and friends who had made loneliness rare. If she were there now, she would be engulfed in loving reassurance instead of sitting by herself, worrying about why she was feeling so strange. Swept by a wave of almost unbearable longing to be with people who cared about her, she brushed away a tear.

Hormonal upheavals notwithstanding, she had to get control of herself. Climbing resolutely back into bed, she switched off the light and wiggled around until she was thoroughly comfortable. But sleep remained elusive. She was still wide awake when at last she heard Adam's key in the door shortly before dawn.

Not bothering with a robe, she raced down the steps to meet him. Despite his obvious exhaustion, he grinned at the sight of her and hugged her close. His overcoat carried the damp chill of early morning. Kate felt it clearly through her thin nightgown and shivered.

Suddenly serious, Adam demanded, "What are you doing up at this hour?"

Reluctant to admit that she hadn't been able to sleep, she shrugged. "Oh, I guess I heard you come in."

He sighed and shucked his coat before drawing her close again. "And I thought I was being so quiet." His lips brushed hers gently as he added, "I'm sorry, honey."

Realizing that he was apologizing for his absence

as much as for waking her, Kate smiled gently. "That's okay. Now come upstairs and get out of those clothes. You must be beat."

"I am, but I can't sleep long. Just a couple of hours."

"Oh, Adam, you can't mean that."

"I'm afraid so. We patched up the problem as best we could, but I've got no confidence that the system will hold once we start it running again. I want to be there to keep an eye on it."

Kate bit her lip. She thought he was foolish to go back to work with almost no sleep, but she also knew it was his choice. She had never been a woman who tried to mother her husband, and she wasn't about to start now.

"All right, tiger," she teased gently. "But let's try to catch a few winks before we tackle the world again."

Adam was so tired that she had to help him pull off his clothes. She forced herself to bite back the impulse to ask him again not to go in early. His head had barely hit the pillow before he was asleep. Snuggled close to him, Kate was at last able to relax. The faintly spicy scent of his skin followed her into her dreams.

Three hours later they were both up and dressed. Except for the shadows beneath his blue eyes, Adam looked as fit as ever. Kate wished she felt the same. She was so tired, she felt numb. The memory of days when she could have gotten by on even less sleep for much longer irked her. When Adam suggested she should stay home from work at least for the morning, she shook her head vehemently.

"Absolutely not. I've got too much to do."

"You won't get it done if you fall asleep at your desk."

"Don't worry. If that happens, Pete will wake me up. He's taken to sticking his head in my office every half-hour or so just to make sure I'm okay."

"Good for Pete. Remind me to thank him next time we meet."

"I'm surprised you haven't insisted he call you with status reports."

"Now there's an idea..."

Groaning, Kate followed him out to the car. She might find his protectiveness a bit hard to take, but she was happier than ever not to have to take the bus. Throughout most of the trip into town, she dozed lightly, and she actually felt slightly better by the time Adam let her off in front of her building.

The day passed in a blur. It took all her concentration to manage even a semblance of alertness. But she must have pulled it off, because no one remarked that there was anything strange about her behavior. Only Pete, who was all too perceptive, picked up on her brittleness and commented on it.

"Late night?"

Kate sighed. She thought longingly of how good it would feel to be still in bed. "'Fraid so."

Pete frowned. "Did you decide you want Willy to be a copywriter after all? With the intensive experience he's getting, he'll be ready before you know it."

Arching her eyebrows, Kate muttered, "I wish I could claim to have been up working, but that wasn't the case." Hesitantly she admitted, "Adam was stuck at the office, and I came down with a classic case of the heebie-jeebies. I couldn't sleep until he got home."

Reassured that she hadn't been deliberately overdoing, Pete's attitude softened. "That's kind of sweet."

"*Sweet?* Bizarre would be more like it. I've never had trouble sleeping when he was away before."

"You've never been pregnant before," Pete pointed out reasonably.

"Don't try to inject logic into this conversation. It would be totally out of place. Anyway, I expect to catch up on the lost hours tonight."

"You can't really do that, you know. Studies show that once you've lost an opportunity for sleep, it can't be regained."

"Since when did you turn into a walking encyclopedia?"

"Sorry," Pete murmured not at all apologetically, "but it's the truth. Why don't you just go home early?"

Kate was tempted, but she stubbornly rejected the idea. "No, I'll wait for Adam. Heaven knows, I've got enough to keep me occupied."

More than enough, actually. But still not so much that she wasn't vividly aware of each passing hour. She was looking at the clock yet again, wondering why the last half-hour before five o'clock was moving by so slowly, when her phone rang.

"It's me," Adam began, the apologetic note in his voice alerting her to trouble. "I meant to call you earlier, but I never got the chance. Things have really been screwed up here all day."

"The computer again?"

"Yes, only now it looks as though we underestimated the original problem. I'm sorry, honey, but I'm

# Gilded Spring

going to have to stay again tonight. We're really in a bind."

But so am I. I need your company, your nearness, your attention. The words stuck in her throat. She couldn't—wouldn't—utter them. It would be unfair to Adam, putting an unwarranted burden on him when he was just trying to do his job. And she would look unforgivably weak and dependent when she was in truth neither.

"All right, I'll take a cab home again."

"Good. And sweetheart..."

"Yes?"

"Make sure you eat a good dinner and get to bed early. I'll try not to wake you when I come in."

He wouldn't have to. She would be awake. But maybe tonight she would be able to pretend otherwise.

"You do that. I'll see you in the morning."

She hung up, silently damning her own weakness. Not too long ago, before she became pregnant, she would have taken his late nights in stride. Now she found herself absurdly tearful at the idea of having to get through another evening without him.

Somehow, without her even being aware that it was happening, she seemed to be evolving into exactly the sort of clinging woman she had always regarded with both pity and contempt. Perhaps she couldn't do anything to change that, but she could sure do her darnedest to keep Adam from finding out. He had enough on his mind without discovering that the woman he had lived with for five years was becoming a stranger even to herself.

Her resolve to hide her true feelings from him was

tested severely through the rest of that week as continued problems at work kept him away from home each evening. Over and over Kate lectured herself about the importance of being patient and understanding. He was exhausted, up against a wall, pressed to his limits. The last thing he needed was her recriminations.

But her resentment grew, and with it came the frightening thought that perhaps Adam wasn't being completely honest with her. What if he wasn't spending his nights at the office with a recalcitrant computer? What if . . .

*Stop that,* her saner self commanded. Not once in five years of marriage had Adam given her the slightest reason to think him capable of infidelity. The fact that she was suddenly capable of suspecting it horrified her. Not only was she becoming a stranger, but this new side of herself wasn't the least bit attractive. She was weak, fearful, doubting—all the qualities she and Adam both despised.

And there didn't seem to be the slightest thing she could do about it. Day followed day, and her bitterness grew. She saw Adam rarely, and when they were together, he was too tired and distracted to sense her mood. For that she was grateful, but not for anything else. Her warm, generous spirit seemed to be withering while she watched. If the present state of affairs continued much longer, all that she valued most in herself was liable to dry up completely and blow away.

The impasse finally reached the inevitable breaking point at the end of the week, when Kate was lying awake yet again in the big bed, listening to Adam letting himself into the house. As always, he came quietly up the stairs and eased the door cautiously open. Slipping inside, he removed his clothes silently and went into the bathroom for a moment, closing the door before turning on the light. She heard water running briefly before he turned off the tap, flicked the switch, and came to bed.

In the darkness of the silent room, she could hear the steady rise and fall of his breathing. She knew he wasn't asleep, but it still surprised her when he murmured her name softly.

"Kate—are you asleep?"

When she didn't answer, he turned over, propping himself up on his elbow. "You aren't, are you?"

"No..."

"Why not?" Before she could answer, perhaps even to tell him the truth, he chuckled softly. "Never mind. I'm too glad that you're awake to quibble about why." Reaching for her, he drew her close to the warm strength of his body.

"We finally licked that goddamn computer. Threatening to turn it in for scrap seems to be what did it. I can still hardly believe it, but by the time I left the office, it had been running perfectly for a good four hours."

"That's nice..."

"Hmmm, you bet it is." His arms tightened, his voice dropping an octave to grow husky and amorous. "Not as nice as the way you smell, though. Or the way you feel." His hands stroked over her gently, cupping her full breasts as he caressed her in the ways he knew never failed to arouse her.

Or at least they had never failed in the past. But then Kate had never been in quite the mood she was that night. Stiffly she drew back from him. "I'm tired."

He didn't seem to hear her. Instead he buried his mouth in her throat and nuzzled her tenderly.

More loudly she repeated, "Adam, I said I'm tired." To give emphasis to her words, she deliberately pushed him away.

He looked at her in bewilderment for a moment before a slow flush stained his cheeks. It was the first time in five years that she had refused to make love with him. Not because there were never times when he wanted to and she didn't, or vice versa, but because when that had happened before they had understood each other's silent signals and had not pursued the matter to the point at which refusal became necessary.

But this time Adam had been too tired and too caught up in himself to sense how she felt. Embarrassed by his lack of sensitivity, he drew back. The look on his face made Kate almost regret her coldness. Almost, but not quite.

As she turned on her side away from him, she reminded herself how little attention he had paid to her in the last few days, despite how much she had needed him. The fact that she hadn't given him much chance to recognize that need did not for the moment penetrate her resentment. She lay awake for a long time before at last falling into an uneasy sleep that did nothing to still her growing sense of vulnerability and insecurity.

## 10

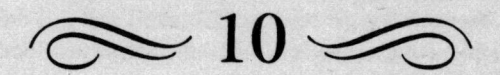

THE FOLLOWING MORNING Kate was in her office, treating herself to what was nowadays a rare cup of coffee, when Lois dropped by. The copy chief was dressed with even more than her usual care. Her thick auburn hair was pulled back in an elegant chignon, and she wore a designer knit dress and jacket that managed to look both perfectly tailored and nicely sexy.

"The Femme meeting didn't get moved up, by any chance, did it?" Kate asked.

Lois nodded wryly. "You guessed it. The grande dame, who has final say on everything the company does, has decided to go into seclusion for a while at her favorite spa. Before that happens we have to get her okay on the copy and layouts. McKay and I are going over there this afternoon. I just wanted to check with you on any last-minute changes."

Kate thought a moment before she said, "I'm really satisfied with the campaign as it stands now. Is there anything you'd like me to rewrite?"

"No, I think it's perfect, and I've had no trouble convincing McKay that he thinks so, too. Now all we have to do is sell the company."

For once Kate was glad of the agency policy that

only top brass made client presentations. In the past she had occasionally resented her exclusion from talks that directly affected the fate of her copy. But now, feeling as tired as she did, she had no desire to attend the Femme meeting. On the contrary, she was looking forward to going home early.

"Good luck with it," she told Lois. "If I'm not here when you get back, I'll look forward to hearing all about it tomorrow."

At her boss's slightly startled look, she laughed. "I know what you're going to say. Not too long ago I wouldn't have dreamed of leaving before we knew the results of that meeting. But frankly, these days I can stand to wait a few more hours. I hope you understand."

"Of course I do," Lois assured her. "In fact, I'm delighted that you're being so sensible. The easier you make things on yourself, the more inclined you'll be to work as close as possible to the end of your pregnancy."

"You can count on that. I've got no intention of sitting home for weeks staring at my tummy and jumping every time I burp."

Lois nodded, making no secret of how pleased she was to hear that her star copywriter wanted to stay on as long as possible. "Have you given any thought to when you'll come back?"

"Not yet," Kate admitted. "The truth is, I'm not exactly looking forward to discussing it with Adam. He's liable to want me to stay home months before the baby comes and not go back for quite a while afterward. We're bound to argue about that, but I'd like to put it off until I'm really feeling up to snuff."

"I take it from what you just said that you don't have any doubts in your own mind about wanting to continue your career."

Kate hadn't envisioned getting into this subject with her boss for some time yet, but she was ready for it. "No," she said firmly, "I don't. That doesn't mean I haven't considered the alternatives. Since finding out that I was pregnant, I've considered everything from coming straight back to work full-time as soon as my maternity leave expires to free-lancing after the baby is born. So far, the only possibility I've ruled out is stopping work entirely. That's definitely not for me."

"Are you sure?" Lois asked quietly.

"Yes, I am. A lot of women are full-time homemakers and that's fine for them, but my objectives and the creative outlets I need are very different. The same is true of a close friend of mine who's expecting her second child. She gave up a very promising career without regrets. I admire her tremendously, but I don't want to emulate her."

"Do you realize that in many ways you're picking the harder road? Trying to combine a career and motherhood is bound to be tough on any woman."

"I know," Kate agreed. "But I've got a couple of pluses on my side. Once I've convinced Adam that I can't be swayed on this issue, I know he'll do everything possible to help me. And I'm in a field where if I find I'm miserable being away from the baby all day, I'll be able to free-lance."

"Absolutely. As your boss, I'm selfish enough to wish you had to stay with this company. But speaking as both another woman and as a friend, I know you won't have any trouble at all setting yourself up as a free-lancer if you decide that's what you want." Hesitantly she added, "There are times when I wish I had followed that route myself. Back when I had an opportunity to do so, there was no support for a woman who wanted to have both a family and a career. I know there are still problems, but I'm glad to see that things have gotten at least a little better."

Lois's candor was both unexpected and heartening. Kate was well aware that many employers would have pressured her to remain on staff full-time. And it might yet come down to that with David McKay. But she was reasonably sure Lois would be able to keep him under control. It was no secret that much of the agency's success was based on its copy chief's superb ability and judgment. The crafty gentleman on the upper floor wasn't likely to threaten such a winning edge by suddenly becoming unreasonable.

For the first time Kate began to consider seriously the possibility of starting her own business after the baby was born. Long after Lois had taken herself off to prepare for the client meeting, she continued to weigh the pros and cons of going independent.

The free-lancers she knew through their work for the agency seemed to fall into two groups. There were the new people who appeared once or twice, and were never seen again because their work didn't meet the agency's standards; and there were the people with personal quirks that made them impossible to get along with.

There was also the smaller but more enduring group of free-lancers that was called in over and over whenever a special touch was needed or the agency staff was simply overwhelmed. Those talented and consistently professional people often made larger incomes than even the best-paid insiders, and they appeared perfectly happy with their chosen approach. In fact, Kate was aware of several people who had been offered choice staff positions, only to turn them down because they valued their independence so highly.

It was something to think about, and Kate did just that all the way uptown to her appointment with Dr. Thorpe. Her checkup went smoothly. The doctor was pleased to hear that the worst of her unpleasant symptoms had disappeared but cautioned her that they might return, if only briefly.

"As I'm sure you've read again and again by now, until you're through the first trimester, we can't be really sure what will happen from day to day. Many of the medications that were once used regularly without a second thought are now banned completely, and the few we have left are used only for emergencies. The best I can do is counsel plenty of rest and patience. If you fall into the pattern set by most women, you'll feel fine through most of your pregnancy."

Kate was willing enough to believe Dr. Thorpe. She only hoped she would get through the first months without any recurrence of the discomfort she had already experienced. As long as she was able to stick to the more moderate schedule she had followed recently, she thought she had a good chance of doing so.

Unfortunately it didn't work out that way. The first indication of trouble came at about four o'clock that afternoon, when she happened to glance out her office window in time to see McKay's limousine depositing the agency head, Lois, and the Femme account executive in front of the building. They were back much sooner than expected, and clearly that was not good news. As the car pulled away, the three people stood on the corner arguing.

The account exec was gesturing wildy, his face red and his usually neat hair mussed. McKay scowled and nodded several times. Lois appeared to be trying to reason with both of them but failing. They were only in Kate's line of vision for a few moments, but it was enough to guess that something had gone very wrong.

Popping her head out the office door, she caught Pete's eye and murmured, "Storm warnings."

He nodded and made a show of draping himself over his desk to hold down the papers and files strewn across it. As Lois swept into the copy department, she spied him and grinned, but only for a moment. By the time she was settled in the chair across from Kate, her expression was somber.

"We've got a problem."

"No kidding. I sort of got that impression from that scene on the sidewalk."

"Oh, you saw that? Good, it saves explaining. To get right to the point, you're too good."

Kate's eyes widened. She had thought for sure her boss was going to say that the client hated her campaign. It wasn't unheard of for even the best efforts to be arbitrarily shot down. She had seen it happen enough times in the past to be inured to it. But this was something different.

"How's that again?"

Lois laughed ruefully. "Madame Lola adores your

approach to Femme. She thinks it is *magnifique* that an American *jeune fille* was able to interpret her own feeling and convictions so correctly. She is *enchantée* with every space ad and commercial. In fact, she is so damn *enchantée* that she's expanding the entire campaign. Our budget is now half again as large as it was."

"But that's fantastic. I don't understand why you look so grim."

"Because, as always seems to be the case in life, there is a catch. Madame Lola is still taking herself off to her spa as planned, and before she goes she wants to see the *entire* campaign. We have forty-eight hours to whip it into shape."

Kate stared at her in disbelief. Lois couldn't be serious. It had taken weeks to prepare the original presentation. Now they had two days to complete half again as much?

There was no need to voice her thoughts. Lois understood them perfectly. She sighed as she said, "All the way back here I tried to talk sense into McKay and that wacko account exec. I explained exactly why we need at least a certain minimum amount of time to prepare a presentation—what goes into it, and so on. You wouldn't think I was telling them anything they didn't already know, but it was still like talking to a couple of eggplants. They won't budge. We have to be back at Femme day after tomorrow with the completed campaign."

"And if it can't be done?" Kate countered.

"Then it can't. We're only human. But frankly, I think this could clinch any plans you have for free-lancing. If you pull this off, you'll be able to write your own ticket with McKay. He'll give you anything you want. Otherwise..."

"It'll be 'So long, honey'?"

"I don't know that for sure," Lois admitted. "He might forgive and forget. On the other hand, he's not exactly the magnanimous type."

Kate didn't have to be convinced of that. She knew that as far as the agency head was concerned, a copywriter was only as good as her last campaign. If he thought she had lost her touch, he wouldn't hesitate to toss her out.

Raising her voice, she called, "Pete!"

Her secretary appeared instantly, creating the impression that he might have been lingering outside the door. His somber look almost wrung a grin from Kate as she said, "Would you please call downstairs for coffee and sandwiches? It looks as though we're going to be here rather late."

He nodded swiftly. "Anything else?"

"Alert the Femme art staff that we have a problem. I'll meet with them in fifteen minutes in the conference room. Also ask the media buyer to stand by, and see if you can round up one or two junior copywriters who would like a chance to strut their stuff. And I would greatly appreciate it if you could stay late. We're really up against the wall."

Pete gave her a look that made it clear wild horses couldn't drag him away. Not for the first time Kate was grateful he enjoyed a challenge as much as she did. She knew his sense of camaraderie and willingness to extend himself to the limit were going to be important to the entire team as the night wore on.

As he started off to carry out her instructions, she called after him, "One other thing. Please get Adam on the phone for me."

Turning back to Lois, she found her boss studying her with admiration. "Whoever said creative types don't make good managers?" the copy chief asked. "You handled that very well."

"Thanks, but that's the easy part. When you're going into a war, the first thing you do is rally the troops."

"True. Now all we have to do is head them in the right direction and get them to the target in time."

Kate grinned. "Madame Lola would undoubtedly be displeased by these military references."

Lois snorted disparagingly. "The old battle-ax would love it. She didn't get where she is today by being a shrinking violet. You should hear her rap out orders. I swear, McKay was positively dazzled."

"Let's just hope he doesn't try to emulate her. That's the one thing that could defeat us before we get started."

Sighing, Lois rose to leave. "I have a sinking feeling McKay is going to hang around and watch us scramble. You know, ever since he became a scout leader, he has this idea he should stay down in the trenches with the troops."

"Is there any way to get rid of him?"

"We could try drugging his coffee."

Kate laughed, but only faintly. She anticipated a long, hard night ahead and didn't appreciate the thought of anything that might make it more difficult.

"Adam's on line one," Pete called.

Lois vanished out the door as Kate reached for the

phone. She took a deep breath, schooling her voice to calmness before she said, "Hi sweetheart. I hope I didn't catch you at a bad time."

"No, everything's fine. What's up?"

"It seems we have a little problem with Femme, so I'm going to have to work late. Don't worry about picking me up. I'll just get a ride home."

Several moments of strained silence passed before he asked, "How late is late?"

Kate wasn't misled by the seeming blandness of his tone. She took a firm grip on her patience. "I'm not sure yet. We have to produce quite a lot of copy in time for a new client presentation day after tomorrow."

She hoped Adam would let it go at that, but he did not. Sharply he asked, "Do you really think it's a good idea to put yourself through so much at this stage of your pregnancy?"

The suggestion that her involvement was voluntary annoyed Kate, especially in light of his own recent expectation that she would understand and accept his late hours without complaint. More pointedly than she had intended, she said, "Being pregnant doesn't exempt me from doing my job. You know that."

"I also know you've had very little sleep recently and that you need a lot of rest. It doesn't make any sense to me that you would put your work before your health."

He hadn't said the baby's health, but as far as Kate was concerned, he might as well have. "You're not being fair, Adam. There's no reason why I can't stay and get this job done without suffering any ill effects."

"How can you be sure of that?"

## Gilded Spring 141

"Because I'm a perfectly healthy woman," she snapped. At the end of a long day, with an even longer night ahead, she was in no mood to listen to his doubts about her ability to juggle pregnancy and a career. Nor did she appreciate the insinuation that she was somehow willing to take risks with the baby.

"Look," she went on irately, "I'm just too busy to get into this right now. You'll have to take my word for it. I'll see you at home."

He started to say something, but Kate quickly hung up. She couldn't remember ever being so abrupt with him before, but neither had she ever felt so provoked.

In the past they had occasionally argued about how much time and attention they were giving to work versus their marriage. They had always smoothed over the conflicts quickly because they each understood the pressures and demands influencing the other.

If all things had been equal, Kate would have tried to make Adam see her point of view. But he had her at a decided disadvantage. She was wearier than she wanted to admit, as well as preoccupied by the Femme problem. And after her talk with Lois that morning, the question of her future was very much on her mind.

She simply had all she could cope with at the moment. It wasn't like Adam not to realize that, but instead he seemed to be thinking only of her pregnancy while ignoring all the other important parts of her life.

Telling herself that made it easier to rationalize her resentment of his attitude. But it didn't stop her from worrying off and on throughout the evening as the copy and art teams scrambled to meet Madame Lola's requirements and the hours ticked past remorselessly.

## 11

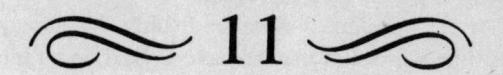

"I CAN'T BELIEVE we actually pulled it off." Pete sighed as he held the lobby door open for Kate. The night guard waved as they left, then went back to his newspaper.

"We don't know Madame Lola will like what we've done," she reminded him as they paused outside the building.

"She'd better, or I will personally drown her in her mud bath."

Kate laughed quietly. The cool night air revived her somewhat. She glanced up the darkened street, struck by how different it looked without the vast hordes of people. Seeing the city when shadows softened the sharp corners of buildings and a gentle wind blew through the glass-and-steel canyons made it vastly more personal, as though a special part of New York belonged only to her.

Pete seemed to feel something similar. Following her gaze, he murmured, "Seeing the city like this almost makes it worthwhile, don't you think?"

*"Almost?"* she teased gently. "You can't kid me. You're nuts about this place."

Pete grinned, his narrow face catching the amber glow of a street lamp. Wistfully he said, "I must be nuts to stay here. If I had any sense, I would have gone back home years ago when I realized I wasn't going to be the next Nureyev."

"But you didn't," Kate said softly. "You stayed, just like the rest of us who have to hold on no matter what."

"That's what makes New Yorkers unique. We're survivors. Whatever fate throws at us, we bounce back." Pete laughed and pulled his jacket closer as a gust of wind off the river struck them. "If all else fails, there's always the good old raspberry."

"I could have used a few of those this evening," Kate admitted. "I came close to braining McKay more than once."

Pete nodded sympathetically. The agency head had distressed them all by insisting on being part of the emergency art and copy meetings that went on far into the night. As if that weren't bad enough, at ten o'clock he apparently decided things weren't going well and began making suggestions about the actual content of the campaign.

Lois had finally managed to distract him by mentioning the awards they might win. Although several shelves were already filled with plaques and statues, McKay still had an insatiable appetite for those tokens of approval given out by their colleagues. Lois kept him preoccupied with rehearsing his acceptance speeches while Kate and the other copywriters hashed out the expanded campaign in time for the art department to complete its own work before the meeting with Madame Lola.

All things considered, Kate was pleased with the results. It never failed to amaze her how talented,

## Gilded Spring 145

motivated people often turned out their best work under the worst circumstances. The members of the small group making their way home at nearly midnight had every reason to feel proud.

"Are you going to take a cab?" Pete asked.

"If I can get one at this hour." Kate doubted she could, but maybe if she walked a block over toward Fifth Avenue...

Pete offered to go with her, but she assured him it wasn't necessary. He was worn out himself and eager to get home. On the brightly lit street checked regularly by patrol cars, she would be fine. Agreeing reluctantly, he left her a few moments later.

Kate stood awhile longer, trying to gather her strength for the journey home. She couldn't remember ever feeling so tired. The excitement of the creative challenge that had sustained her so far was disappearing rapidly, leaving in its wake a profound exhaustion. Her body trembled with fatigue, and she had trouble even seeing straight.

Sighing, she reminded herself that she wouldn't get home by standing where she was. Doggedly putting one foot in front of the other, she began heading toward Fifth Avenue and the taxi she hoped to find.

The car came at her out of nowhere. One moment the street was quiet and dark, the next the glare of headlights blinded her and the shriek of tires resounded down the street.

Kate took an instinctive step back, her throat tightening painfully as all the air rushed out of her. She had barely a moment to realize what was happening before the driver slammed to a stop beside the curb and the door on the passenger side swung open.

Visions of terrifying crimes she had read about in the papers or seen on television raced through her mind. She was too far from the building lobby for the watchman to hear anything, and Pete was long gone. There was no one in sight to call for help. Screaming would be useless.

Only one thought penetrated the red mist of her fear: *run!* Turning to flee, she was stopped by a shockingly familiar voice.

"Get in the car," Adam demanded.

Frozen in place, Kate stared at him in disbelief. She was at once infinitely glad to see him and furiously angry. The two emotions warred for an instant before anger won.

"How *dare* you pull such a stupid stunt! You scared me half out of my mind!"

Far from looking repentant, Adam's features merely darkened. So softly that she had to strain to hear him, he repeated, "I said to get in the car."

The stubbornness that was an intrinsic part of her nature, and which almost always worked to her own good, suddenly showed a different side of itself. Her back stiffened as a dull flush stained her cheeks. She was damned if she'd let him first terrify and then bully her.

"Go to hell." Turning, she began walking swiftly down the block away from him.

She got no further than a couple of yards before powerful hands gripped her. Swinging her off her feet, Adam carried her purposefully back to the car and deposited her none too gently in the passenger seat.

Pride prevented her from protesting further against what she obviously could not prevent—and the fact that some deeply rooted instinct warned her that Adam had been pushed to the breaking point. She had no desire to find out what he would do if she tried to get away from him again.

Neither of them said a word all the way home. Adam drove with single-minded concentration, never once glancing at her. Kate stared out the window, trying not to think about what was happening between them.

In her exhausted state she was also very vulnerable. Tears glistened in her eyes, but she resolutely blinked them back. No matter what, she wouldn't let him see how miserable he was making her.

As Adam parked the car, she fumbled with the seat belt. Anxious to get away, she found her fingers stiff and clumsy. She was still trying to work the buckle when Adam came around the front of the car, opened the passenger door, and flipped open the recalcitrant clasp. As he stood aside waiting for her to get out, Kate stole a look at him.

The stark desolation in his eyes struck her like a blow. She came very close to reaching out to him right then and trying to smooth over the conflict that had erupted so unexpectedly between them. But the unyielding determination she also saw in his expression stopped her cold. Adam was clearly not prepared to relent. And she had no strength to argue with him.

Upstairs in their bedroom, she got out of her clothes quickly and slid under the covers. The tense silence continued to stretch between them as Adam joined her and snapped off the light. Long minutes passed before Kate drifted into an uneasy sleep.

She woke the next morning feeling as though she

had not rested at all. Her head throbbed, and her eyes burned. Remnants of uneasy dreams followed her into consciousness. She turned over quickly, only to see that Adam's side of the bed was already empty.

Rising, she pulled on a robe and padded downstairs. It was so quiet that she wondered if he had already left for the office, despite the fact that it was only a little after six o'clock. But that thought vanished when she peered into the kitchen and found him slumped over the butcher-block table.

He looked every bit as unhappy as she felt. Beneath the night's growth of beard, his face was unnaturally pale. Thick chestnut hair fell in unruly strands across his brow. His piercing blue eyes were rimmed with red, and his broad shoulders were bowed in an attitude of dejection she had never seen in him before.

Hesitantly she took a step forward. "Adam . . . ?"

He raised his head slowly, as though he was reluctant to look at her. "What is it?"

"Are you—all right?"

For a long moment he did no more than stare at her. She had to resist the urge to retreat from the chilling scrutiny that made her feel like a butterfly pinned to a board.

Just when she thought she couldn't bear it a moment longer, Adam said, "No, I'm not anything like all right. I've been sitting here trying to figure out how a woman I thought I knew can suddenly decide to put the demands of her career ahead of her unborn child."

Kate recoiled inside. The accusation, so quietly uttered, reverberated through her. She wanted desperately to believe that she had heard him wrong, even though she knew she had not.

"H-how can you say something so horrible? You know I'm not doing anything of the kind."

"All I know is that you're apparently unwilling to make a single concession to your condition. You expect to go right on as though nothing has changed, and the baby be damned."

"That isn't true!"

"Isn't it? I saw you last night. You were wiped out. A good stiff wind could have knocked you down. Any pregnant woman with half an ounce of sense wouldn't have subjected herself to that. But no—you had to prove you're still the best no matter what."

They were both standing now, facing each other, staring at each other remorselessly. Kate's hands clenched into fists at her sides as she insisted, "I don't have to prove anything. Not to you or to anyone else. I've set my own standards for too long to start changing them now just because my husband has decided that having a baby should turn me into a vegetable!"

"Hah! That's exactly what I mean. You can't give an inch. Not to me or the baby, not even to yourself. You've been so obsessed with your goddamn career, you've forgotten how to care about anything else."

The blatant unfairness of his accusations made her gasp. What about all the caring that had gone on for the last five years? What about all the times she had compromised in the interest of making their marriage a success? What about the demands of his own career, which showed no sign of lessening despite his impending fatherhood?

His willingness to ignore all that reaffirmed Kate's belief that he wasn't interested in anything except the baby. Painfully bewildered by his actions, she told herself he was at last showing his true colors. All that business about being supportive and understanding was just so much nonsense. When it really came down to it, he expected her to turn into a baby-making machine without so much as a murmur of protest.

Stiffly she said, "You've got a hell of a nerve to bring this up when you haven't shown the slightest interest in me or the baby because you were too busy nursing a sick computer!"

When he tried to answer, she held up a hand angrily. "I'm not finished. There's no way I'm even going to try to guess what's making you behave like this. But I'm not going to put up with it. You have no right to say I don't care about you and the baby when you know the opposite is true. And you especially don't have the right to suggest I'd do something to harm our child when you know I'm incapable of such a thing. Later on, when you're feeling more rational, if you want to talk about what's really bothering you, I'll be glad to listen. But until then, just keep your thoughts to yourself."

Turning quickly so that he wouldn't see the tears in her eyes, she returned to the bedroom and got dressed. When she came back downstairs, she could hear the shower going in the guest bathroom. Unwilling to face him again so soon, she left to catch a bus to work.

The day dragged by. Despite the constant stream of last-minute problems and details that she had to attend to before the Femme presentation would be complete, Kate found it impossible to put the scene

## Gilded Spring 151

in the kitchen out of her mind. Over and over she replayed what they had said to each other, growing more and more baffled by both Adam's behavior and her own.

Honesty forced her to admit that there had been wrong on both sides. Certainly he shouldn't have said what he had, but her anger made her forget what a fundamentally kind and decent man he was. She would have done better to try to talk out their problems right then. In certain situations it was wise to wait and let emotions cool down before attempting to resolve the problem. But she had the sinking feeling that this situation might not be one of them.

The memory of how Adam had looked the night before and again that morning made her realize that without even meaning to, she had hurt him as deeply as he had hurt her. She couldn't bear to think what would happen if the pain they both felt was allowed to fester.

Whether because of her worry over Adam or because of the nonstop pressure in the office, by afternoon she was exhausted. She debated only a moment before deciding it was time to give up for the day.

Lois came into Kate's office just as she was closing her briefcase. "I wanted to double-check the color separations on the ad—" she began before breaking off abruptly. Her eyes darkened with worry as she said, "Kate, you look worn out."

"I am. So if you don't mind, I'm going home."

She trusted Lois to understand that the polite phrasing was strictly a formality. There was simply no way she was going to run the risk of somehow harming the baby by letting herself get any more tired than she already was. Fortunately her boss not only understood but agreed completely.

"Of course, you go right ahead. Everything's under control now, so there's really no reason for you to hang around."

Kate nodded. She greatly appreciated Lois's consideration, even though she was well aware that it would have been a very different story if she had insisted on leaving early the day before.

Now that the worst of the emergency was over, her presence wasn't really vital. But as a senior agency copywriter, she would have been expected to do whatever was necessary to rescue Femme without regard for any personal problems. The question of how she would manage once the baby arrived and demanded her time and attention as well rose again to worry her just when she was least able to cope with it.

By the time she got home, she had considered the problem over and over and had no hope of resolving it. Kate yearned to discuss the matter with Adam, who was, after all, her best friend. She had long ago grown accustomed to asking his advice on a vast range of problems that had cropped up in the course of their personal and professional lives. He did the same with her, and their mutual support was often enough to help them overcome even the most difficult challenges.

But she wasn't about to reveal her fears to the harsh stranger she had glimpsed the previous evening and that morning. Until they could patch up their differences and smooth over the harsh words they had exchanged, she would keep her distance.

That still left her with the problem of needing someone to talk to. Glancing at the clock, she realized that Davey would still be at day school. Maybe Carol would have a few minutes to chat.

The moment she got Carol on the phone, Kate realized it would be impossible to hide the real reason for her call. Carol was too perceptive not to recognize how upset she was.

"Are you home?" Carol asked quickly. "You sound as though you should be."

"I'm curled up in bed with a banana and a glass of milk. How's that for behaving myself?"

Carol laughed softly. "My heavens, is this the real Kate Remington I'm talking to? Or did the advertising world suddenly declare a holiday?"

Though Carol's tone was light, Kate couldn't help but be taken aback. Did she really come across as so completely dedicated to her career that her friends were startled when she took a few hours off?

Slowly she said, "No, I just felt really worn out, so I thought I'd come home early."

"How did they take that at the office?" Carol asked, no hint of humor left in her voice.

"Oh, there wasn't any problem about it. Of course, if it had happened yesterday when we were all in a panic, it would have been a different story." Reluctantly she added, "I'm beginning to see some big problems ahead if I try to keep up the same pace at work after the baby is born."

Carol was silent for a moment before she said gently, "Don't hate me for saying this, but it's perfectly normal for you to start having doubts about your ability to juggle a career and motherhood. I don't know any working woman who's had a baby without going through that."

"Did you?"

"I sure did. And in my case I had already made the decision to take off several years, so it was really a question of how to keep giving my work everything it deserved until I delivered."

"That sounds awfully familiar," Kate admitted.

"I can imagine. We've been conditioned to think we should be able to have a baby without our careers being affected in any way. It would be nice if that were true, but it isn't. You can only cut yourself up into so many little pieces before something has to give."

Wiggling down further in the bed, Kate sighed. "I just can't accept the idea that I may have to give up something I've worked so hard for simply because I'm having a baby."

"Of course you can't. It was tough enough for me to leave a job that was exciting but didn't really mean all that much to me. I can well understand that you don't want to lose something you really enjoy. But who says you have to? All that's really necessary is compromise."

"That's what I'm hoping," Kate said. "But I'm still not sure how to go about it."

"Maybe you shoud start with the premise that it isn't just up to you. Adam will have to accept some changes too, and so will your employer."

Kate couldn't bring herself to admit that Adam was in no mood to accept anything she might suggest. Fortunately Carol didn't press the point. They talked awhile longer before Carol sensed the growing weariness in Kate's voice and encouraged her to get some sleep.

"If it's any consolation to you," she said, laughing, "during my third month with Davey, I dozed off in the middle of a meeting that included the president of the network."

Kate giggled, conjuring up the image of McKay's expression were she to do the same. Somewhat to her surprise, since she was not used to taking naps, she had no trouble following Carol's advice. The muted sounds of children coming home from school filtered through the open windows as she drifted off.

## 12

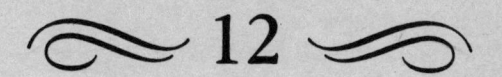

"OH, MR. REMINGTON," the elderly secretary called as Adam strolled by, "there are several messages for you." Handing him the sheaf of slips, she added, "One was from your wife. How is she feeling these days?"

Adam frowned slightly, regretting that in the heady joy of first discovering he was going to be a father, he hadn't hesitated to let everyone in the office know about it. Now he wished he hadn't said a word.

"Uh—she's fine. Did she say why she was calling?"

"Only to tell you that she was leaving the office and you shouldn't bother to pick her up." The secretary smiled as she spoke. "I hope she's all right. She sounded very tired when she called."

Adam stared at the message, not sure how to interpret it. Did Kate actually mean she was going home early? And if so, why? Might she be deliberately trying to prove the unfairness of his accusations by suddenly behaving reasonably? But he had to admit that that just wouldn't be like her. No matter how angry she was at him, she wouldn't do something so petty.

Though he was tempted to call home immediately to find out what was going on, he hesitated. He didn't want to wake her if she was asleep, and he wasn't eager to resume their conversation of that morning. At least not until he had a chance to sort out his own feelings and motivations.

Why on earth had he said those awful things to her? If anyone had told him a few months ago that he would accuse his pregnant wife of not caring about their child, he would have laughed it off as impossible. Yet he had done exactly that, and in the process he had hurt Kate deeply.

Even as he had heard himself claiming that she was only concerned with her career, he had known it wasn't true. Certainly she had every right to be proud of her professional accomplishments. She had worked damn hard for everything she had. But that didn't mean her priorities were screwed up. He knew better than anyone how immensely giving she could be. There wasn't the slightest reason to believe their child wouldn't benefit from the same loving spirit that had so often comforted and helped him.

So why had he lashed out at her?

No more accustomed to deciphering his own feelings than most men, Adam was nonetheless trying to do just that when his secretary buzzed on the intercom to tell him that his brother was calling.

Picking up the phone, Adam smothered a rueful laugh. Trust Brandon to choose this moment to get in touch. The extraordinary empathy that had first developed between them when they were children, and that had grown even stronger over the years, seemed unchanged by the miles that separated them. Adam wasn't at all surprised when his brother skipped the usual chitchat and got right to the point.

"How's Kate?"

"Is that why you called?" Adam hedged. "To check up on your gorgeous sister-in-law?"

"Of course. You don't think I'd call just to talk to you, do you? Now quit fooling around and tell me how she is."

"What's the point? My guess is you've already got a pretty good idea."

Brad sighed softly. "I was hoping I was wrong. Want to tell me about it?"

"There's not much to tell. I acted like an absolute clod, and she's quite rightly angry at me. I was just sitting here trying to figure out what the hell was going on with me when you rang."

"Is it really that bad?"

"Judge for yourself. I told her I thought she cared more for her career than for the baby."

Brad whistled softly. "How come all of a sudden you turned into Mr. Insensitive?"

"Beats me... It's just that this pregnancy business is a lot more complicated than I expected. Fair warning, little brother. What may be as easy as rolling off a log for the birds and the bees gets quite a bit tougher when you're dealing with human beings."

A low laugh reached him along the phone line. "Especially human beings of the female persuasion?"

"You got it. Although, to be honest, I don't think I'm coping nearly as well as Kate is, and she has the much harder part."

"Yeah, but she doesn't have Jell-O for brains."

"Thanks."

"What are brothers for?" Brad countered, ignoring Adam's sarcasm. "Look, you and Kate have as solid a marriage as anyone can hope for. Surely you can work this out."

Adam sighed deeply and ran a hand through his already tousled hair. "We have to, don't we? After all, with a baby on the way, this is hardly the time for a falling out."

"Yeah, but even just considering the two of you, you'd want to patch this up, wouldn't you?"

"Of course I would, but that's the whole point. We can't only consider the two of us anymore. The baby changes everything."

Even as he spoke, Adam knew he was edging up on whatever it was that was really bothering him. Slowly he added, "Nothing's going to be the same anymore, not with the responsibility of a child."

There was silence for several moments before Brad murmured, "Is that what's bugging you, Adam? That you're not going to be able to cope with the responsibility?"

"Our parents sure as hell didn't."

"What's that got to do with you?"

"Come on, Brad. How the hell do I know that I'll be a better father than our old man? Maybe there's more of both him and Mom in me than I want to realize."

"Funny that you haven't shown any sign of it in thirty-five years. I seem to remember you were the guy who held me together after they drank themselves to death and we got shuffled around all those foster homes. You had to do a fair amount of fathering until I got my own act together, and you never let me down. So why are you worrying about how you'll be with your own kid? You'll do fine."

## Gilded Spring

"I don't know..."

"I'll bet it's the part about it not being just the two of you anymore that's really got you tied in knots. Kate's a very special woman. Who could blame you for having mixed feelings about sharing her with anyone?"

"Even our own child?"

"Anyone," Brad repeated firmly. "Look, I can't claim to have any experience in this area, but if you've got half the sense I think you do, you'll let her know what's going on in your head. Kate loves you. She'll understand."

Adam wasn't so sure. After all, how could she understand what he didn't understand himself? Preoccupied with his thoughts, he said good-bye to Brad and hung up.

Kate had gotten pregnant so quickly after they'd made the decision to start a family that he hadn't had a chance to get used to the idea before it had become a reality. And he'd been completely unprepared for the more difficult side effects of childbearing. When he considered how weak and sick she looked sometimes...

It didn't help at all to remember that millions of women around the world were going through exactly the same thing at that very moment. Kate was different. She was his closest friend and lover, a vital part of his life, the woman he depended on in more ways than he could probably ever name. But lately she seemed so far away.... Between her demanding career and the miracle going on within her, there didn't seemed to be much of her left for him.

Was that why he had wanted to make love with

her so often lately? He couldn't deny that in recent weeks their intimacy had always been at his urging. Besides the fact that he simply found her condition enormously exciting sexually, it was also as though he needed to reaffirm their closeness in the most fundamental way possible.

Sighing, Adam leaned back in his chair. He stretched his long legs out in front of him and rubbed his chin absently. Introspection was hard work. No wonder he'd generally avoided it. Where was he... Oh, yes, he loved Kate, but he was still a little shocked by her pregnancy, and he felt sort of left out.

Was that it? He hoped not. It sounded so petty. Imagine what Kate would say if he complained about not being able to share her morning sickness and fatigue.

He backed up a bit and sidled around the idea. Maybe he didn't just feel left out. Maybe he was actually jealous... and scared... *Now wait a minute. Jealous* sounded a lot worse than *left out*. What kind of guy would actually regret not being able to be pregnant? That went against his most deeply rooted ideas about masculinity. Of course, over the years he'd discovered that more than a few of those ideas were dead wrong, and he'd discarded them without regret. It seemed, though, that a few had hung on.

He'd get back to *jealous*. What about *scared?* Certainly he was afraid for Kate. He dreaded the thought of her in pain and couldn't bear to imagine what might happen if there were problems during the delivery. Never mind the incredibly low incidence of maternal mortality; when it was his wife who might be endangered, the odds didn't mean anything.

## Gilded Spring

There was nothing he could do about that fear except read the books, go through the Lamaze course, and pray. But there was another kind of fear gnawing at him that he might be able to deal with. As he had admitted to Brad, he was worried about the impact the baby would have on their marriage.

A wry smile touched his lips as he realized it was his turn to be told that something was perfectly normal. At least the book he was reading on becoming a father said so. Not that it helped. He still felt like a callous idiot for entertaining the merest hint of resentment when he thought he should feel only pride and joy.

Adam shook his head angrily. He was letting himself get trapped in a maze of thoughts of how he *ought* to behave instead of concentrating on his true emotions. Okay, so he was worried about what would happen after the baby arrived. Why?

He must be getting the hang of this soul-searching business, because he found the answer to that one right off the bat. Kate already seemed to have all she could handle and maybe a bit more. There was no way she was going to be able to manage after the baby was born unless she took time and attention away from some other area of her life.

As far as he could see, there were only two possibilities: her job or their marriage. Call him a chauvinist boor, but he was damned if he wanted to see their relationship suffer because she put her career first. Determination stiffened his features, only to dissolve as honesty forced him to admit that Kate wasn't likely to do any such thing.

In the five years they had been together, he had

certainly learned to trust her more than that. There was nothing screwed up about her priorities. She was an intelligent, talented woman with a satisfying job that naturally meant a great deal to her. If the truth be told, she was probably as concerned as he was about how she would cope once the baby arrived.

Which brought him back to Brad's advice that all they needed was to talk.

Having come to a better understanding of what was going on inside his own mind, he was both ready to apologize for what he had said that morning and eager to determine how they could help each other through the coming months.

Putting on his jacket, he headed home, hoping to find Kate awake.

## 13

"Kate, I'm home."

Adam's voice reached Kate through the fog of an uneasy sleep. She turned over restlessly. Part of her wanted to stay where she was, to avoid having to face him. She had no way of knowing what his mood might be. Was he still angry, still ready to hurl ugly words at her?

She could hear him moving around in the kitchen and guessed that if he thought she was asleep he would not disturb her. But what would be gained by that? She couldn't put him off forever.

Impatiently she got out of bed and put on a robe. The sooner they talked, the better. He meant far too much to her to let disagreements fester between them.

Still not quite awake, she started down the stairs. Her mind was on reassuring memories of his tenderness and passion, of the wonderful times they had shared highlighted by their mutual love for the child she was carrying. She was paying little attention to what she was doing as her feet flew from one step to the next.

A dozen steps from the bottom her foot caught in the hem of her robe. She pulled it away impatiently, realizing too late that she had lost her balance. A surge of disbelief shot through her. Grabbing for the handrail, her fingers closed over air. She tried again, only to miss the railing by inches. Her stomach clenched as a strangled scream was wrenched from her throat.

Horror hit her like a frigid wave, sweeping her into a grotesque world where simple, ordinary things were twisted into terrifying mockeries of themselves. Time stretched into seemingly endless seconds. For an agonizing instant she seemed to be suspended in air. Then, with terrifying reality, the hard, unyielding floor rushed up at her, and she landed in a crumpled heap at the bottom of the stairs.

Adam was at her side before she could even lift her head. His face was pale with concern as he bent over her, his voice shaking. "Kate, are you hurt?"

"I—I'm not sure—" Hesitantly, fearful of what she might discover, she took inventory of her body. The arm she had fallen on throbbed painfully but didn't seem to be broken. Her left ankle felt as though it had been twisted, but not all that seriously. There was a faint ringing in her ears, but it went away even as she noticed it. Hardly daring to believe that she might have come through the accident with no greater injury, she murmured, "I—I seem to be all right..."

The words had barely left her when a searing, twisting contraction arched through her abdomen. She screamed in an agony of the heart that had nothing to do with mere physical suffering.

*"Oh, God—please no—the baby—"*

Adam's arms closed around her convulsively. His body bent over her in a futile effort to shield her from what was happening. His cheeks were wet with tears that merged with her own. Lifting her, he carried her

# Gilded Spring

up the stairs to their room and laid her on the bed.

Struggling desperately to control his own terror, he reached for the phone. His fingers fumbled with the buttons. He started over, only then remembering that he didn't know the number. Cursing, he threw down the receiver and reached for the phone book, ripping pages in his haste.

Tabot Fish Store...Tamale Heaven...Teardrop Optometrist... *Sweet God in Heaven, where was the damn number?*

*Thorpe, Dr.* Breathing hard, he punched the buttons. Endless seconds passed before the call went through. It rang once, then again. A receptionist answered.

He made no effort to be polite, simply barked out his demand to speak with the doctor at once. Belatedly he feared the woman would take offense and keep him waiting. But she didn't hesitate. Dr. Thorpe came to the phone immediately.

"Keep her very quiet, Adam. I should be there in twenty minutes." He barely had a chance to acknowledge her instructions before she had hung up.

Turning back to Kate, he found her face ashen and wet with tears. He took a deep breath and tried to keep his voice steady but failed. "The doctor's on the way. She said to stay right where you are and not move until she gets here." The words almost choked him. They were shallow comfort to offer in the face of such fear.

Kate nodded abjectly. The pillow beneath her head was damp with tears. The silk robe clung to her perspiration-soaked body. Vaguely she realized that the brief pain that had stabbed through her was not followed by others, but that thought brought scant reassurance. Never in her life had she confronted such unrelenting misery. Not all her strength and pride combined were equal to it.

"Adam—" She moaned softly. "I tripped—it was an accident—"

"I know, honey," he murmured. "Just lie still now. The doctor will be here soon."

"No—you don't understand. I was so happy—I knew everything was going to be all right after we talked. I wanted to tell you how foolish I felt for worrying about what would happen to my career after the baby came. All we needed to do was make a few compromises...everything seemed so right..." Her voice broke. Another spasm passed through her, making her writhe, leaving her more fearful than ever.

Adam tilted her head back enough to take in the tear-washed anguish of her eyes and the twisting pain that marred the smooth line of her mouth. His throat tightened. "Don't try to talk, sweetheart. You have to save your strength. Everything will be fine—you'll see."

Distracted, Kate moved her head from side to side on the pillow. "You're not listening...please...you have to understand what I'm trying to tell you. *It wasn't my fault!*"

Adam's lips parted soundlessly. His eyes blazed for a moment before softening with an undefinable emotion that made her breath catch. What little color was left in his face vanished completely.

"My God—is that what this is all about? You're afraid I'll blame you if you—lose the baby?"

Swallowing convulsively, Kate nodded. She was

beyond denial, beyond reticence. All her emotions were raw and exposed. It would take very little for him to snap the last remnants of her self-control completely. "You warned me. You said I was working too hard—said I didn't care. But it wasn't true! I did care—I do—so much. You can't know—"

"No," Adam murmured, so softly that she could barely hear him. "I can't know. When it comes to understanding what it means to have a human being growing inside you, I can't begin to grasp the enormity of it all. But that doesn't make any difference."

Trembling, he cupped Kate's face in his hands, beseeching her to believe him. "Kate, I love you, more than I think you'll ever know. Certainly I love our baby, too, and I want it to be safe. But you're the one who really counts. Without you—"

He stopped and took several deep breaths before he could continue. "I can't even cope with the thought of being without you," he said finally in a strangled voice. "You're everything to me, just by yourself. I was wrong to say what I did. The words came from bewilderment and jealousy. But they don't change the fact of how much I love you. Just you. Completely apart from the baby, your career, everything."

Kate heard him without fully absorbing the utter sincerity of what he said. She knew only that the wonderful man she loved more than life itself was struggling to repress his own fear and grief for her sake, and the knowledge was bitter. "Oh, Adam... I'm such a coward."

His mouth trembled, then steadied with an effort as he said, "You? You're the bravest person I know."

"How can you say that? Look at me, crying and

helpless and all. When I should be strong—"

"For God's sake, Kate! I'm not some—some casual lover you can't allow past your defenses. I'm your husband. I'm not going to judge you, no matter what!"

"But you want the baby so much—"

"No more than you do. If the worst happens, we'll both suffer. But we'll do it together." A tiny, infinitely tender smile curved his lips. "Don't try to tell me you haven't noticed that's what being husband and wife is all about. Maybe we lost sight of it for a short time, but that doesn't make it any less true. Together we can face anything."

His voice dropped slightly, his hand brushing the tears from her cheek. "We've been lucky so far, Kate. All the time we've been married, we've pretty much gotten what we wanted. This is the first time we've come up against something we simply can't control. Whatever's going to happen to the baby, we can't do anything more to stop it than we already have. But we can have a big impact on what happens afterward. No matter how this turns out, we'll help each other through it."

His words washed over her like a soothing balm. Some of the agonizing tension slipped away from her. She relaxed slightly, though her hands still gripped his tightly. They remained close together on the bed through uncounted minutes until the peal of the doorbell drew them apart.

"I'll be right back," Adam promised as he hurried from the room. True to his word, he returned in moments with Dr. Thorpe. Kate was every bit as relieved to see him as she was to see the physician. Even the short time without him had been agonizing.

# Gilded Spring

"Kate," the doctor said softly, "I understand you tripped and fell down those stairs out there." She inclined her head toward the corridor. "Did you fall all the way down?"

"No, about a dozen steps—I think. Not more."

"Did you lose consciousness?"

"No, I'm sure about that. I felt dazed and there was a ringing in my ears, but that's all."

"And now how are you feeling?"

"Bruised...scared...what does it matter? All that counts is the baby. I've had two—contractions, I guess, since I fell."

Nodding quietly, the doctor sat beside her on the bed and took her hand, unobtrusively gauging her pulse and skin temperature. Adam stood to one side, out of the way but still close by. He made no offer to leave, and neither of the women suggested he should.

"How far apart were the pains?"

"Several minutes...I can't say for certain..."

"How long ago was the last one?"

"Five minutes...maybe ten..."

"Longer than the interval between them?"

"Yes—yes, I'm sure of that."

Dr. Thorpe smiled gently. "Good. Now let's just see if I can get some idea of what's going on in there." She put her hand on Kate's slightly swollen abdomen and left it there as she continued to talk to her reassuringly.

"I know you've had a terrible scare, and I'm not going to lie to you. You may lose the baby because of that fall. But it isn't inevitable—not considering how you are right now. So let's just take it a step at a time and see what happens. All right?"

Kate nodded mutely. All her attention was focused inward on the mysterious workings of her body. After long moments she said, "I—I don't think anything's happening."

"I think you're right," the doctor agreed quietly. "But it's early yet to be sure. I'll tell you what. Why don't you go into the bathroom and check to see if there's any sign of bleeding."

As Kate began to sit up, Adam stepped forward quickly. Without a word he lifted her in his arms and carried her across the room. When he set her down near the sink, she thought he meant to leave, but instead he stayed where he was.

She turned away, unable to face him at such a moment. "The doctor said to check—"

"I heard her."

"Please..."

He hesitated, not wanting to leave her. Only the anguish in her eyes forced him to do so. Reluctantly he stepped just outside the partly open door, listening intently to every sound Kate made. The relieved sigh that broke from her found its echo in him.

When they returned and told the doctor that there was no bleeding, her professional detachment slipped just enough to reveal a relief almost as profound as their own. She smiled as Adam helped Kate back into bed. "It does look as though you may get lucky. But that doesn't mean all the danger is over. You're going to have to take it very easy for the next few days."

She paused, as though expecting to be asked exactly what that meant or for how long the restrictions would apply. But Kate said nothing. Of course she was going to take it easy. If Dr. Thorpe told her not to move out of bed for the next six months, she wouldn't budge an inch. If she prescribed gallons of molasses and castor oil to offset the effects of the fall, she would swallow every drop without a murmur. If she advised a steady diet of radishes and sauerkraut, then so be it.

The capricious fate that had threatened her baby was going to face more of a fight than it might have expected. Nobody and nothing was going to take Willy away from her without an all-out struggle.

While Kate remained silent, Adam asked detailed questions concerning her care so that he would be sure of doing everything possible to help both her and the baby.

Dr. Thorpe's instructions were simple and to the point. Kate could get up to go to the bathroom; otherwise she was to remain in bed. She should eat as much good, nutritious food as she could comfortably hold and drink plenty of liquids. Above all, she must not worry. Mental exertion was every bit as bad as physical strain. She could work, but at the slightest sign of fatigue she was to stop and rest.

Adam took careful note of everything the doctor said and then escorted her downstairs. As she left, Dr. Thorpe cautioned him to call her at the slightest sign of a problem.

"Kate's a perfectly healthy young woman, Adam, but she's had a bad shaking up. Don't hesitate to let me know if anything happens."

More grateful than he could express for the doctor's care, Adam agreed quickly. He saw her to her car before returning immediately to Kate's side. Sitting down on the edge of the bed, he took her hand in his and managed a shaky smile. "Sounds like you're grounded for a while."

"That's fine with me. I'm just so glad that—" She couldn't go on. Fresh tears welled up in her eyes. She tried to brush them away, but Adam took her hand in his.

With infinite gentleness he wiped her cheeks dry and touched a tender kiss to her lips. Huskily he whispered, "Everything's going to be fine, sweetheart. You'll see. Now you should try to sleep."

Kate didn't need any further encouragement. Her lids felt weighted by lead bricks. The warmth of Adam's closeness wrapped her in loving comfort as she drifted off.

Twice in the night she woke, starting back to consciousness in sudden fear as the memory of falling down the stairs crashed in on her. Each time she found Adam still awake beside her. Each time his arms encircled her gently, and his softly murmured words of reassurance eased her back into sleep.

When she woke in the morning, he looked as though he had not slept at all. His eyes were red-rimmed, his hair mussed, and his face shadowed by a night's growth of beard. He had forgotten to undress, and his once crisp shirt and slacks were limp and wrinkled. Smiling tenderly, Kate murmured, "It looks like you've been working on a new old bum outfit."

Touching a hand to her face as though needing to convince himself that she was really there and safe, Adam laughed shakily. "Every man needs a versatile wardrobe." They stared at each other in silence for a long moment before he asked, "How are you feeling?"

She thought about that for an instant, assessing the

signals her body was sending her. "All right... I think. A little sore, but otherwise fine." Her smile grew more confident. "I'm starved, though."

His relief was so profound that she could almost sense it reaching out to envelop her. "Now that I can do something about. Give me a few minutes, and I'll whip up the best breakfast you've ever had."

Before he went down to the kitchen, he helped her into the bathroom and waited while she freshened up. Tucked back into bed with strict orders not to move, Kate grinned at him impishly. "That doesn't include phone calls, does it?"

"I suppose not," he allowed. "Just don't talk to anyone who's liable to upset you."

Having promised faithfully not to, she shooed him out of the room, then dialed Lois's office. When the copy chief answered, she explained briefly about what had happened. The older woman was deeply concerned, but finally accepted Kate's assurances that so far she seemed to be getting off lightly. After learning that the revised Femme campaign had won raves from Madame Lola, she arranged to have work sent home to her. They chatted for a few minutes longer before she hung up, just as Adam returned with their breakfast.

The tray was laden with blueberry muffins, scrambled eggs, sausage, orange juice, and even a pot of the decaffeinated coffee she had recently begun drinking. As he set the tray down carefully beside her, she laughed softly. "Good lord, who else is coming to breakfast?"

"Nobody, and I'm going to sit here until you eat every scrap."

"If I do that, I won't be able to move for a week!"

"That," he informed her, "is the idea."

In the end they compromised. Adam shared the meal, and Kate did her best to eat a good portion of it. She had to admit that everything tasted delicious. Perhaps because she had come so close to tragedy the night before, all her senses seemed vividly alive. She was acutely aware of the sunlight streaming through the windows, the chirping birds, the scent of daffodils in a vase beside the bed.

But her attention focused most clearly on Adam. Even as rumpled and worn out as he was, he seemed the most glorious sight in all the world. He was strong, intelligent, tender, and as vulnerable in his own way as she was in hers. Their spirits spoke to each other at levels that went far beyond the boundaries of any single time or place. Apart, they lost an essential part of their very souls. Together, they could face anything.

His words of the night before echoed in her mind. She finally understood what they meant. Marriage didn't mean sharing just the good times and the successes. It meant triumphing over all the differences, disagreements, and misunderstandings, all the petty confusions and frightening problems of everyday existence. It meant creating a haven of love and peace that remained with them wherever they went and whatever might happen to them. Most of all, it meant having the courage to admit how much they needed each other, even when such dependency could open the way to pain and loss.

She put a gentle hand on her bulging abdomen, smiling as she did so to let him know that nothing was wrong. The baby had already given them so much. All they could offer in return was the simple gift of life.

Kate's eyes closed for an instant as she breathed a silent prayer. When she opened them again, she found Adam watching her. His gaze was so tender that she knew she had not prayed alone. Their hands met across her body.

Whatever happened—tomorrow, next month, fifty years from now—they would face it together.

# Epilogue

IT WAS VERY quiet in the room. Adam stood up and stretched slowly. He couldn't remember ever being so tired, or so exultant.

Staring out the window, he was barely aware of the snowflakes drifting by. New York was in the throes of a Christmas blizzard, but as far as he was concerned, the sun was shining brightly.

A smile touched his mouth as he turned back to look at Kate, fast asleep in the hospital bed. He walked over to her and stared down at the features he knew better than his own. It seemed incredible that he could detect no sign of the trial she had passed through.

Ray had been right. None of the classes and reading had prepared him for the experience of childbirth itself. As long as he lived, he would never forget his anxiety when Kate had woken him at dawn and announced calmly that her labor had begun.

He grinned wryly, knowing that he had been a classic expectant father as he tried to rush her off to the hospital at once. She had matter-of-factly ignored him and gone about getting dressed. She'd taken a final look at a free-lance assignment that was due that day and even touched up her nail polish, because she was determined to look as good as possible when their child arrived.

He'd been close to exploding by the time she had finally agreed to get into the car. The trip to the hospital had seemed endless, even though traffic had been unusually light. Dr. Thorpe had met them in the homey birthing room they were to occupy. She had checked Kate over, left a few instructions, and gone off to visit another patient with a dry comment that babies always seemed to know when it was a holiday and arrived just in time to share the fun.

Amanda Katherine Sherri Remington had certainly chosen a good time to make her entrance into the world. Pink and squalling, she had emerged just before sunset, as all the Christmas lights were coming on along the avenues and the first soft snowflakes were beginning to fall.

Kate had been fully conscious and able to share in the wonder of their daughter's birth. There had been tears in her deep brown eyes and a wide smile on her face as she watched Adam hold the baby even before the cord was cut. When he had laid the tiny, perfect body at her breast, the three of them had been joined in a circle of love that nothing could ever break.

Adam bent closer now, peering at the wrinkled, red face in the cradle next to the bed. Amanda Katherine Sherri Remington, alias Willy, was going to be a beauty. He was sure of that, even if no one else but her mother could see it. Very carefully, so as not to disturb the baby, he covered her up more securely.

Sitting down beside the bed, he gazed protectively

at the newborn child in the cradle and the lovely young woman dreaming peacefully nearby. A well-meaning nurse had suggested he go home, but Adam saw no reason to do so. He was already there.

# NEW FROM THE PUBLISHERS OF *SECOND CHANCE AT LOVE!*

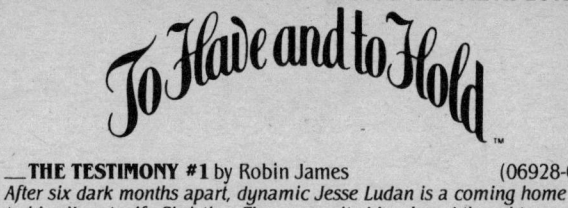

## To Have and to Hold™

___ **THE TESTIMONY #1** by Robin James  (06928-0)
*After six dark months apart, dynamic Jesse Ludan is a coming home to his vibrant wife Christine. They are united by shared thoughts and feelings, but sometimes they seem like strangers as they struggle to reaffirm their love.*

___ **A TASTE OF HEAVEN #2** by Jennifer Rose  (06929-9)
*Dena and Richard Klein share a life of wedded bliss...until Dena launches her own restaurant. She goes from walking on air to walking on eggs—until she and Richard get their marriage cooking again.*

___ **TREAD SOFTLY #3** by Ann Cristy  (06930-2)
*Cady Densmore's love for her husband Rafe doesn't dim during the dangerous surgery that restores his health, or during the long campaign to reelect him to the Senate. But misunderstandings threaten the very foundation of their marriage.*

___ **THEY SAID IT WOULDN'T LAST #4** by Elaine Tucker  (06931-0)
*When Glory Mathers, a successful author, married Wade Wilson, an out-of-work actor, all the gossips shook their heads. Now, ten years later, Wade is a famous film star and Glory feels eclipsed...*

___ **GILDED SPRING #5** by Jenny Bates  (06932-9)
*Kate yearns to have Adam's child, the ultimate expression of their abiding love. But impending parenthood unleashes fears and uncertainties that threaten to unravel the delicate fabric of their marriage.*

___ **LEGAL AND TENDER #6** by Candice Adams  (06933-7)
*When Linny becomes her lawyer husband's legal secretary, she's sure that being at Wes's side by day...and in his arms at night...can only improve their marriage. But misunderstandings arise...*

___ **THE FAMILY PLAN #7** by Nuria Wood  (06934-5)
*Jenny fears domesticity may be dulling her marriage, but her struggles to expand her horizons—and reawaken her husband's desire—provoke family confusion and comic catastrophe.*

**All Titles are $1.95**

Available at your local bookstore or return this form to:

**SECOND CHANCE AT LOVE**
Book Mailing Service
P.O. Box 690, Rockville Centre, NY 11571

Please send me the titles checked above. I enclose _____. Include 75¢ for postage and handling if one book is ordered; 25¢ per book for two or more not to exceed $1.75. California, Illinois, New York and Tennessee residents please add sales tax.

NAME_____

ADDRESS_____

CITY_____STATE/ZIP_____

(allow six weeks for delivery)                                    THTH #67

# DON'T MISS THESE TITLES IN THE SECOND CHANCE AT LOVE SERIES

### STRANGER IN PARADISE #154
### by Laurel Blake
Nicole Starr managed the Seawinds boutique very well without Grant Sutton's expert advice. Now he is determined to change much more than just her business practices...

### KISSED BY MAGIC #155
### by Kay Robbins
In a whimsical conspiracy, company president Rebel Sinclair temporarily assigns her power to Donovan, her male secretary. Is his sudden—and outrageous—seduction really to win her heart...or her chain of hotels?

### LOVESTRUCK #156
### by Margot Leslie
He's a tall, blond stranger who calls her Lady Luck. She's a promising playwright revising her script for Broadway. From the first, their onstage antagonism sparks offstage passion...

### DEEP IN THE HEART #157
### by Lynn Lawrence
Carrie Chandler arrives in rugged west Texas in search of a rare antique locomotive. But in Bat Bartholomew's powerful embrace she finds something of far greater value...

### SEASON OF MARRIAGE #158
### by Diane Crawford
Julie Logan's coveted assignment to interview reclusive vintner Jonathan Brook precipitates a professional crisis... and personal heartache...when she falls in love—then learns the secret behind his initial hostility...

### THE LOVING TOUCH #159
### by Aimée Duvall
Cassie's new boss at the Albuquerque City Zoo sends her senses reeling! Inadvertently she sets off one comical mishap after another...until Paul finally holds her close...

## WATCH FOR 6 NEW TITLES EVERY MONTH!

## Second Chance at Love

- ___ 06540-4 **FROM THE TORRID PAST #49** Ann Cristy
- ___ 06544-7 **RECKLESS LONGING #50** Daisy Logan
- ___ 05851-3 **LOVE'S MASQUERADE #51** Lillian Marsh
- ___ 06148-4 **THE STEELE HEART #52** Jocelyn Day
- ___ 06422-X **UNTAMED DESIRE #53** Beth Brookes
- ___ 06651-6 **VENUS RISING #54** Michelle Roland
- ___ 06595-1 **SWEET VICTORY #55** Jena Hunt
- ___ 06575-7 **TOO NEAR THE SUN #56** Aimée Duvall
- ___ 05625-1 **MOURNING BRIDE #57** Lucia Curzon
- ___ 06411-4 **THE GOLDEN TOUCH #58** Robin James
- ___ 06596-X **EMBRACED BY DESTINY #59** Simone Hadary
- ___ 06660-5 **TORN ASUNDER #60** Ann Cristy
- ___ 06573-0 **MIRAGE #61** Margie Michaels
- ___ 06650-8 **ON WINGS OF MAGIC #62** Susanna Collins
- ___ 05816-5 **DOUBLE DECEPTION #63** Amanda Troy
- ___ 06675-3 **APOLLO'S DREAM #64** Claire Evans
- ___ 06689-3 **SWEETER THAN WINE #78** Jena Hunt
- ___ 06690-7 **SAVAGE EDEN #79** Diane Crawford
- ___ 06692-3 **THE WAYWARD WIDOW #81** Anne Mayfield
- ___ 06693-1 **TARNISHED RAINBOW #82** Jocelyn Day
- ___ 06694-X **STARLIT SEDUCTION #83** Anne Reed
- ___ 06695-8 **LOVER IN BLUE #84** Aimée Duvall
- ___ 06696-6 **THE FAMILIAR TOUCH #85** Lynn Lawrence
- ___ 06697-4 **TWILIGHT EMBRACE #86** Jennifer Rose
- ___ 06698-2 **QUEEN OF HEARTS #87** Lucia Curzon
- ___ 06851-9 **A MAN'S PERSUASION #89** Katherine Granger
- ___ 06852-7 **FORBIDDEN RAPTURE #90** Kate Nevins
- ___ 06853-5 **THIS WILD HEART #91** Margarett McKean
- ___ 06854-3 **SPLENDID SAVAGE #92** Zandra Colt
- ___ 06855-1 **THE EARL'S FANCY #93** Charlotte Hines
- ___ 06858-6 **BREATHLESS DAWN #94** Susanna Collins
- ___ 06859-4 **SWEET SURRENDER #95** Diana Mars
- ___ 06860-8 **GUARDED MOMENTS #96** Lynn Fairfax
- ___ 06861-6 **ECSTASY RECLAIMED #97** Brandy LaRue
- ___ 06862-4 **THE WIND'S EMBRACE #98** Melinda Harris
- ___ 06863-2 **THE FORGOTTEN BRIDE #99** Lillian Marsh
- ___ 06864-0 **A PROMISE TO CHERISH #100** LaVyrle Spencer
- ___ 06866-7 **BELOVED STRANGER #102** Michelle Roland
- ___ 06867-5 **ENTHRALLED #103** Ann Cristy
- ___ 06869-1 **DEFIANT MISTRESS #105** Anne Devon
- ___ 06870-5 **RELENTLESS DESIRE #106** Sandra Brown
- ___ 06871-3 **SCENES FROM THE HEART #107** Marie Charles
- ___ 06872-1 **SPRING FEVER #108** Simone Hadary
- ___ 06873-X **IN THE ARMS OF A STRANGER #109** Deborah Joyce
- ___ 06874-8 **TAKEN BY STORM #110** Kay Robbins
- ___ 06899-3 **THE ARDENT PROTECTOR #111** Amanda Kent

All of the above titles are $1.75 per copy

SK-41a

___ 07200-1 **A LASTING TREASURE #112** Cally Hughes $1.95
___ 07203-6 **COME WINTER'S END #115** Claire Evans $1.95
___ 07212-5 **SONG FOR A LIFETIME #124** Mary Haskell $1.95
___ 07213-3 **HIDDEN DREAMS #125** Johanna Phillips $1.95
___ 07214-1 **LONGING UNVEILED #126** Meredith Kingston $1.95
___ 07215-X **JADE TIDE #127** Jena Hunt $1.95
___ 07216-8 **THE MARRYING KIND #128** Jocelyn Day $1.95
___ 07217-6 **CONQUERING EMBRACE #129** Ariel Tierney $1.95
___ 07218-4 **ELUSIVE DAWN #130** Kay Robbins $1.95
___ 07219-2 **ON WINGS OF PASSION #131** Beth Brookes $1.95
___ 07220-6 **WITH NO REGRETS #132** Nuria Wood $1.95
___ 07221-4 **CHERISHED MOMENTS #133** Sarah Ashley $1.95
___ 07222-2 **PARISIAN NIGHTS #134** Susanna Collins $1.95
___ 07233-0 **GOLDEN ILLUSIONS #135** Sarah Crewe $1.95
___ 07224-9 **ENTWINED DESTINIES #136** Rachel Wayne $1.95
___ 07225-7 **TEMPTATION'S KISS #137** Sandra Brown $1.95
___ 07226-5 **SOUTHERN PLEASURES #138** Daisy Logan $1.95
___ 07227-3 **FORBIDDEN MELODY #139** Nicola Andrews $1.95
___ 07228-1 **INNOCENT SEDUCTION #140** Cally Hughes $1.95
___ 07229-X **SEASON OF DESIRE #141** Jan Mathews $1.95
___ 07230-3 **HEARTS DIVIDED #142** Francine Rivers $1.95
___ 07231-1 **A SPLENDID OBSESSION #143** Francesca Sinclaire $1.95
___ 07232-X **REACH FOR TOMORROW #144** Mary Haskell $1.95
___ 07233-8 **CLAIMED BY RAPTURE #145** Marie Charles $1.95
___ 07234-6 **A TASTE FOR LOVING #146** Frances Davies $1.95
___ 07235-4 **PROUD POSSESSION #147** Jena Hunt $1.95
___ 07236-2 **SILKEN TREMORS #148** Sybil LeGrand $1.95
___ 07237-0 **A DARING PROPOSITION #149** Jeanne Grant $1.95
___ 07238-9 **ISLAND FIRES #150** Jocelyn Day $1.95
___ 07239-7 **MOONLIGHT ON THE BAY #151** Maggie Peck $1.95
___ 07240-0 **ONCE MORE WITH FEELING #152** Melinda Harris $1.95
___ 07241-9 **INTIMATE SCOUNDRELS #153** Cathy Thacker $1.95
___ 07242-7 **STRANGER IN PARADISE #154** Laurel Blake $1.95
___ 07243-5 **KISSED BY MAGIC #155** Kay Robbins $1.95
___ 07244-3 **LOVESTRUCK #156** Margot Leslie $1.95
___ 07245-1 **DEEP IN THE HEART #157** Lynn Lawrence $1.95
___ 07246-X **SEASON OF MARRIAGE #158** Diane Crawford $1.95
___ 07247-8 **THE LOVING TOUCH #159** Aimée Duvall $1.95

---

*Available at your local bookstore or return this form to:*

**SECOND CHANCE AT LOVE**
*Book Mailing Service*
*P.O. Box 690, Rockville Centre, NY 11571*

Please send me the titles checked above. I enclose _____. Include 75¢ for postage and handling if one book is ordered; 25¢ per book for two or more not to exceed $1.75. California, Illinois, New York and Tennessee residents please add sales tax.

NAME _____

ADDRESS _____

CITY _____ STATE/ZIP _____

(allow six weeks for delivery)    SK-41b